Revolution's Horizon
Scott Kinkade

Cover by Ramon MacAirap (monmacairap@gmail.com).

This book was edited by Cathy Lopez (cvlopezediting@gmail.com).

Prolog

October 8, 1916 (Infini Calendar), Beelitz, Germany.

The man from the Bavarian Reserve Infantry Regiment 16 lay convalescing in the hospital room with all the other wounded soldiers. He had been lucky to survive what many European soldiers considered to be a death sentence: the dropping of a British bomb onto his dugout near Bapaume.

Dozens of beds filled the room, each one containing an injured German soldier, most of whom had been far less lucky than him. All things considered, he had gotten off lightly.

The various nurses made their rounds to distribute morphine to the ailing men. He hoped one would get to him soon as his leg ached furiously from the exploding shell. It had been bandaged properly, although numerous red splotches marred the wrapping.

He was proud to have been wounded in service to the great German cause. He hoped to be able to return to duty as soon as possible.

He closed his eyes to try and get some rest but the shuffling of feet next to his bed woke him. A nurse he had never seen before stood there. "Lance Corporal Adolph Hitler?" she said in German.

"Yes," he said wearily.

"Good," she said. "You are the right person." She proceeded to hook something up to his IV.

He studied her for a moment. She had black hair with scattered gray strands and appeared to be in her late forties or early fifties. She held a determined expression much as the greatest soldiers

1

had. She tensed as she fiddled with a bag of emerald liquid. "That's not morphine," he said.

"No," she replied. She then leaned in closer and whispered, "It is what you deserve."

By now, the strange liquid was flowing into his arm. Alarmed, he said, "Who are you?"

"I'm the opposite of you."

Suddenly, he was paralyzed. Unable to move a muscle, he could only gawk in terror as the mysterious woman stared venomously at him. "You are a disgrace to Austria," she continued.

Who was this woman and why did she seem to hate him more than the British did?

His heartbeat had been racing the past thirty seconds, but now it gradually slowed.

"Be thankful I'm being merciful," she said.

At that moment, he could find nothing to be thankful for.

Part 1

Dobro pozhalovat' v Rossiyu, tovarishch

[Welcome to Russia, Comrade]

Glava 1

The New York Chronicle
"Civil Unrest in Russia Causes Worry"
By Nelly Flowers

It has been over two years since the nation of Russia entered the Great War. Since that time, the proud country has suffered greatly. As of this writing, over one million soldiers have been killed in battle, and food shortages continue to cause skyrocketing prices. Tsar Nicolas II has repeatedly come under fire for his insistence on dragging his people into the most devastating conflict the world has ever seen.

He has drawn further ire with his seemingly blind devotion to the Siberian peasant Grigori Rasputin. The controversial *starets* [holy man] had increased his influence over the country in recent months before his abrupt disappearance. The tsar and his wife Alexandra seemed hellbent on punishing anyone who questioned the so-called mystic.

The Bolshevik party, led by Vladimir Ilyich Ulyanov—more popularly known as Lenin—have had enough. Keeping Bloody Sunday in their minds—an event where Imperial soldiers fired upon peaceful protestors—they have now forced the tsar to abdicate the throne. As of last week, the royal family has been moved to Yekaterinburg nearly 1,200 miles to the east.

However, the Bolshevik forces are divided on ideology. Lenin has the Red Army, while the anti-communist White Army opposes them. Even now, the Whites are marching on Petrograd with their ultimate goal being to reach Yekaterinburg and free the royal family.

But the question remains as to how the Whites are so well-equipped. Yes, they have "appropriated" equipment and weaponry, yet is that enough to maintain their momentum? A series of early defeats should have ended their campaign, but they remain stronger than ever. Rumors persist of a shadowy backer pulling the strings from behind the scenes. If true, one should find it alarming that a major military force can be manipulated to someone else's ends.

This reporter will continue to investigate this claim and will keep you all apprised of the goings-on in Russia.

* * *

Nelly sat back in her rickety wooden chair that looked like it would collapse from a feather landing on it. Bundled up in her thick beige coat to protect against the vicious Russian weather (even indoors), she yearned for this conflict to be over.

She currently sat in a trailer being pulled through the streets of Petrograd by a diesel-powered truck. The trailer measured six feet wide, eight feet tall, and 12 feet long. It bounced up and down as it traversed the rocky city roads.

In front of her was a metal brick about four feet high and six feet long. Imbedded in the center of the brick was a black screen with the green words she had just finished typing on the keyboard below. This was the Scribemeister, a machine that took in words and converted them to electronic signals which would then be slingshot back to America where a similar device would receive them at the newspaper's office.

At forty years old, Nelly had seen more excitement in her life than most people could even fathom. When she was only thirteen, she had been kidnapped, caught in an aeroship explosion, kidnapped *again*, taken to a secret prison in Death Valley, transported to a world of the human subconscious called Pleroma, undergone a trial to unlock the hidden power of the human brain, and finally transported again to the Unassigned Lands where she had almost been sucked up by a tornado during the Land Run.

And yet, she had never seen a conflict like the one that now raged throughout Europe. No doubt this would have pleased that monster Garasheth had he still been here to see it. She wondered briefly what Michael Lazarus must have thought about this. No doubt it must have been a crushing blow to his spirit after they had all fought so hard to prevent the Gnostagar from taking mankind down this exact path.

She sighed. Garasheth's faction may have been defeated, but perhaps there was no saving humanity from itself.

Suddenly, words appeared on the screen in front of her:

Good job, Nelly. Your family wants to know
when you're coming home. I told them
hopefully soon. They miss you.

She smiled. The message was from her editor
who was very glad he didn't have to come out here to
report on Russia's strife. Her thoughts then turned
to her husband and son who both lived in Queens.
She had named her son Michael Evan Jay
Rosenbaum after the compatriots she had shared
her earliest adventure with. He wasn't a girl, so she
couldn't name him "Eva," but she figured "Evan" was
close enough. She missed her family so much that
the urge to flee her duties and return home
sometimes came over her. Reason always won out,
thankfully.

The voice of Sam, her assistant and driver,
came in through the trailer's tinny speakers. "Nell, I
found us a secluded place along the river. We can
stay here tonight."

The trailer came to a stop and the brilliant
glow of the setting sun painted a magnificent picture
above the beautiful blue of the Baltic Sea.

She stepped outside into the frigid Russian
air. Ice particles sparkled in the twilight. They had
parked on the Marakova Embankment, and to the
north, she could see the island of Ostrov Petrovskiy
a thousand feet away.

Sam exited the truck and came over to join
her. "I should have known. The weather report called
for balls-freezing cold." He was ten years her junior,
with short, cropped brown hair and an average build.
He, too, was bundled to the gills.

"I know," Nelly said, laughing, "with a chance
of hellish frostbite."

He shrugged and smiled. "Welcome to Russia, comrade."

Her smile abruptly evaporated. "Are you sure we couldn't get a hotel?"

Shaking his head, he replied, *"Nyet.* Lenin and his boys aren't too keen on Americans. We could get locked up as spies. The White Army is a tad more accommodating, but also real trigger-happy. It's best for both of us if we stay incognito, and that means *Le Chalet Trailer."*

She sighed. "But it's soooo cold."

"Oh? I didn't realize you Oklahomans were such tenderfeet. Didn't you have to fight for survival growing up on the reservation?"

She had to roll her eyes at this. "It wasn't a *reservation*. It was the Unassigned Lands. My parents and I participated in the Land Run. And, I'll have you know, we barely dodged a tornado. It just wasn't so dad gummed cold as this."

"Careful with that language, missy! I may have to report you if you keep on being vulgar."

She laughed again. "Go ahead! See if Peterson can find someone else dumb enough to come all the way out here just to keep Americans informed about world events."

Sam poured on the smugness. "He found me, didn't he?"

"Honestly, why *did* you volunteer for this?"

"Good question." He leaned in closer. "Maybe I'm a sucker for a pretty face." He leaned out.

More eye-rolling. "I'm a *married* face, Samuel Granger. And last I checked, you only went for blondes."

He threw up his hands. "Fair enough. Maybe I just like your personality."

"I believe that more than you liking this wrinkled, old face."

"I count exactly five wrinkles, so quit complaining," he said, still smiling. He began making his way around the truck, checking to make sure the wheels weren't stuck in the snow. They never knew when they'd have to make a quick exit from the scene.

"If I feel like complaining, that's exactly what I—"

Her words were cut off by a faint rumbling under her feet followed by a steadily increasing hum in the air which jostled the packs of snow on the ground

"What's that?" Sam asked.

They both looked around. At first, there was nothing to see. But then Nelly noticed dozens of lights in the sky to the northwest coming towards them. They could only be one thing. "Aeroships!"

"Yeah, but *who's* aeroships?" Sam said.

"Think about it! They're coming in from White Army territory. The Reds can't fly there because of the Tesla Towers, so it must be the Whites. They're coming to take Petrograd."

"That's crazy!" Sam said as he came back around to join her. "Petrograd has Tesla Towers. The Whites will be shot down as soon as they get within range."

As if to challenge his declaration, a series of explosions rocked the city. One boom after another, accompanied by fire and smoke hurtling into the air, took down the majority of Tesla Towers around them. The smell of acrid smoke and burning metal greeted Nelly's nose.

"Unless, of course, that happens," she said.

The familiar white of the aeroships' hulls came into view. Shrill air raid sirens generated a vile cacophony across Petrograd. This soon became grotesquely intermingled with the crackling of arcs

9

of white-hot electricity being emitted from the aeroships' cannons. Red Army installations were cooked instantly, and a chorus of screams filled the oncoming night.

"We need to leave!" Nelly said emphatically.

It was then that the White Army aeroships reached their position. It was also then that she realized they were parked next to a Red Army-controlled building.

She was about to warn Sam when cascading arcs of electricity rained down upon their position from one of the aeroships above them. She ran to push Sam out of the way, but an arc shot down and engulfed him. She watched in slow motion as his skin turned from white to brown to deep black. His mouth opened wider than should have been possible for a human, but she couldn't hear anything over the whine of the militarized lightning.

And then, it was over. The aeroship moved on and the charbroiled husk that had been Sam Granger fell to its knees and then onto its stomach. Except, there was no stomach anymore, only a blackened skeleton. The sickening stench of charred flesh turned her stomach inside out, and she emptied it all over the ground. Nelly Flowers spent the next few moments expertly multitasking both crying and vomiting.

But she knew she couldn't remain there. The White Army invasion had only just begun. She needed to get out of the city, and that meant going southeast.

She hopped into the cab of the truck only to find the keys weren't in it. She realized with crushing horror that Sam had them. With that in mind, she got out and tiptoed to his corpse, spying nothing but fried bones. Panic set in as she decided the keys must have been destroyed. She was now stuck in a city under siege.

She turned every way she could trying to decide where to go. She went one way, then changed her mind and went the opposite way. She did this for several moments until her foot sent something skidding across the ground. It was the keys! Sam must have tossed them—voluntarily or otherwise—when he had been struck.

She had a chance now.

She snatched up the keys—wincing at the heat of them—and took off her coat. She wrapped it around Sam's skeleton and put it in the trailer. She then got back in the cab. The diesel engine started up without a hitch and she hit the accelerator, shooting off along the Marakova Embankment towards the Dvortsovyy Most bridge.

Unfortunately, the rest of the traffic along this particular road had the same idea. Nelly careened around cars trying to escape the White Army. By now, the sun had set entirely, and most of the lighting in the city came from burning buildings that cast an eerie glow.

More deadly arcs began striking the ground all around her. She didn't know who exactly the Whites were targeting, but she was caught in the crossfire, nonetheless. A few cars up ahead got struck and promptly went out of control, hit the guardrails, and dove into the Neva River.

A collision accompanied by a blinding flash rocked the cab. The truck had been struck, but it was of an old design, hardy and resistant to electricity.

Within a few moments, she arrived at the Dvortsovyy Most bridge and headed southeast over the river. She quickly realized this might have been a mistake as at the other end was the Winter Palace—and a barricade composed of cars and short, metal walls that had no doubt been set up to defend against the Whites. With armed guards ahead and aeroships behind and above, she decided she would be tempting fate no matter what she did, and just kept heading forward.

When she was a few hundred feet away from the barricade, the guards behind it began shooting. The gunfire instantly carved numerous spider web cracks into the wind shield, prompting her to duck. The truck swerved slightly as she could no longer see properly to keep it straight.

When she was twelve, she had passed out from the punishing force of the abrupt deployment of a parachute high above the Mississippi River. The crash she now felt when her truck slammed into the barricade was comparable and brought back unpleasant memories. Her head collided with the vehicle's dashboard hard enough to make her vision flash with a sickening white light.

Something wet trickled down her forehead, but she had no time to check her condition. Sitting upright, she spied the Winter Palace—or two of them. Nelly blinked a few times to clear her vision, and then she could see the magnificent building to her left.

More pops of gunfire, along with the *tink-tink* of bullets pelting uselessly against the solid frame of the trailer, resounded somewhere in the back of her mind. Her thoughts were akin to a mountain, with the soldiers and bullets situated along the base. The top of the mountain, and that which currently commanded her attention, was getting past all of this and surviving to return home to her family. Blood crept down into her right eye, making it even more difficult to see.

Suddenly, the charred corpse of Sam came up the other side of the mountain and stood prominently on top with a grotesque grin. *What will I tell his family? What could possibly justify dragging him out here?* True, it hadn't been Nelly who strong-armed Sam into coming to Russia; it had been Peterson who had insisted on her being accompanied by a capable man. Her previous question returned to her unbidden: *Why did you volunteer for this?*

Glava 2

The Neva River, the next morning.

He had been having the worst dream of his life. His trusted friends had lured him to their house and fed him cakes. After he ate them, he had begun to feel sick. His friends then revealed their true intentions and pulled pistols on him. He had tried to run but bullets exploded out of his chest.

His last memory was of being thrown into the river.

Suddenly, Grigori Rasputin's eyes shot open to a murky scene. He realized he was underwater. He tried to move his limbs but found it difficult. Realization hit him again—a good portion of his body had frozen.

He must be in the Neva, he thought. His icy restraints kept him prisoner for the moment, but nobody had ever accused Grigori Rasputin of being weak. He was a man of God, after all.

He closed his eyes and began praying. After a minute of this, he let divine light into his being and, with a primal roar, commanded his body into action, easily shattering his frozen shackles. Then, remembering he had been underwater for who knew how long, he raised his head above the surface and took the deepest breath of his life.

Rasputin howled with laughter when he saw he had drifted to an embankment. Those fools! They thought they could kill a man who walks hand-in-hand with God. They thought they could kill the friend of the tsar and his Empress. He shook violently from the cold, but his spirit was warmed by the knowledge that traitorous cur Felix Yusupov and his accomplices would receive the harshest possible punishment for their sins.

He staggered up the embankment but collapsed at the top along a winding street. Good, he thought—he was still in Petrograd. He recognized the area as being not far from Yusupov Palace.

Felix Yusupov was a Russian aristocrat who had befriended Rasputin, but the latter now realized he was just as wicked as everyone else who questioned the Siberian holy man. This was not the first attempt on Rasputin's life, but it was certainly the most dramatic and by far the closest to succeeding.

As he sat on top of the embankment, he considered his next move. The first order of business was getting someplace warm. God's grace kept him alive, but he would still be weak until he received warmth and nourishment. Then he would send a telegram to *Tsarkoye Selo* where the royal family lived and tell them about Yusupov's heinous act.

* * *

Rasputin found a nearby kitchen factory with adequate heating and sat down at a table in a rickety chair. These places were essentially massive mess halls set up in old factories.

He put his head down on the wooden table and immediately lost consciousness. He dreamt of a pale monster that was coming for his beloved Romanovs. The creature sought young Anastasia's brain to devour. He shuddered when he awoke hours later. What manner of fiend would target the grand duchess? He had to move quickly to save her.

Thankfully, this particular establishment had a Scribemeister machine in the back, and he strode over to it feeling much better physically. "Boy!" he shouted to the teenager sitting at the console. "I wish to send a message to the royal palace at Tsarkoye Selo. I must warn the tsar about a dangerous plot."

"Where have you been, old man?" the kid replied. "The Bolsheviks dethroned the autocracy and put a provisional government in charge."

"What nonsense is this?" he yelled.

"The only thing that doesn't make sense here is you, mister. The Romanovs have been imprisoned at Ipatiev House in Yekaterinburg. Everyone in Russia knows that."

Flummoxed, Rasputin scoured the cavernous space for a newspaper. When he found one, it confirmed the boy's story. A lot more time had passed than the holy man had realized. In his absence, a new regime had arisen, and his dear friends had fallen from grace. His hands trembled violently with every word he read.

Finally, he threw down the paper in disgust and set off toward the nearest train station. He would go to Yekaterinburg, a distance of some 2,220 kilometers, and save the royal family himself.

* * *

The skies above Petrograd.

General Lavr Kornilov sat in his private cabin aboard the aeroship *Belyy Terror* waiting for his daily call with the person supplying the White Army with weapons and equipment. He alone knew this person's identity. To the rest of his men, their mysterious benefactor was known only as the *Prokrovitel,* the Patron.

Kornilov was the de facto leader of the White Army, but in reality, he took orders from the

Prokrovitel who had their own interest in the civil unrest within Russia.

Born in Kazakhstan in 1870, he was a thin man in his late forties now. He had a mustache that formed an arrow pointing up toward his head. His vaguely Oriental eyes betrayed his Turkish ancestry.

There was a desk in his cabin with a circular imprint on the top for transmissions. He stared impatiently at it, wanting very much to get this over with and get on with the rest of his day. There was still much to be done despite having just taken Petrograd although they had taken the Reds completely by surprise, and that put a smile on his otherwise stern face.

Suddenly, the perimeter around the circle lit up a series of fluctuating colors. He pressed a button behind it on the desk, and a vaguely human shape appeared above the circle. The image was scrambled by design in case anyone walked in on them, resulting in distorted human proportions. The Prokrovitel demanded tight security.

"Update," they ordered in a distorted voice.

He cleared his throat. "We have taken Petrograd. This has been a great victory for the true servants of Russia, and it is all thanks to your generosity."

"Quit smiling," they said. "You are moving far too slowly, and we are running out of time. You must make haste to Yekaterinburg and secure Anastasia Romanov."

"It is not that simple. There are thousands of kilometers between here and there that must be traversed, along with a legion of your Tesla Towers."

"The towers are of no consequence, provided you did as instructed and left one of the Reds' standing."

"I did," he confirmed.

"Good," the Prokrovitel said. "I'm sending you a data card that you will insert into the central terminal inside the tower. It will infect all the other towers with an electrical worm and shut them all down. Once that is done, you must proceed at top speed toward Yekaterinburg."

He nodded. "Understood. However, I need your assurance you will continue to support our cause of bringing democracy to Russia after we have upheld our end of the deal."

"I assure you, General, with what you're giving me in return, it will be well worth it to continue assisting you."

"Very well," Kornilov said. "But we cannot simply race across thousands of kilometers at breakneck speed. We would quickly over-extend ourselves and become easy prey for Lenin's forces."

But the Prokrovitel said, "Don't worry, General. I will provide you with enough resources to overcome the Reds. All I want in return is Anastasia Romanov."

"Does she really have the powers you claim?"

"That is not your concern. Just bring her to me as soon as physically possible."

"For the sake of Russia, it will be done."

"Good." Suddenly, the Prokrovitel began coughing violently. "I remind you—there isn't much time."

The holo-projector powered down and the conversation was over.

* * *

Ipatiev House.

The screams of the teenage boy gradually faded to a dull groaning while his sister waved her hands over his body. He currently lay on his bed in his private bedroom within their house prison in Yekaterinburg east of the Ural Mountains.

The boy was Alexei Nikolaevna the tsarevich which, up until recently, meant he would one day rule Russia. However, the Bolsheviks—leading the Red Army—had cruelly ousted the royal family and imprisoned them here.

More importantly, though, Alexei was a hemophiliac, a fact that had been closely guarded by his parents as it was considered disgraceful to have such an illness within such a distinguished bloodline. And today he had been having one of his episodes, each of which caused him unbearable agony.

As his older sister, Anastasia used her powers—presumably given to her by God—to ease his pain. The 17-year-old grand duchess loved all her family dearly, and she did all she could to help them during this difficult time. No one knew when they would be released and allowed to return home to Tsarkoye Selo.

When she was younger, she and her older sisters had put on plays for the family to entertain them and cheer them up when things were bad. And things had certainly been bad during the Great War, with everyone blaming Papa for all their problems. Eventually, they turned against him even though he had been chosen by God to rule.

And now, here they were.

"It hurts," Alexei said, his voice strained. Sweat covered his head, and he clutched his sheets in a death grip. Thankfully, his breathing was becoming less labored as the minutes passed.

"I know," Anastasia said.

In the beginning, all she could do was keep her brother from bleeding to death from minor cuts. But as time went on, her powers had grown, and she was confident one day she could cure Alexei's hemophilia entirely.

Mama stuck to the belief his savior was Uncle Grigori, that creepy holy man. Anastasia always found him repulsive. His long beard was hideous and much too long, and he didn't bathe nearly enough for her liking. But it was those eyes that disturbed her most. He always seemed to be staring into her soul. He had convinced her parents he was the one saving Alexei, no matter how often she protested the opposite. Her power was invisible and only she could see the waves of whitish-green energy radiating out from her palms, so Uncle Grigori's claims had more weight to Mama and Papa.

But Uncle Grigori had been murdered not long ago. Despite everything, she felt bad for him. Mama had been enraged when she found out; the Empress had always referred to him as "Our Friend" and had been extremely overprotective of him. The authorities had exposed Felix Yusupov and his friends as the culprits, but Felix fled to France before he could be arrested.

The door to the room opened behind her. "Still at work, *Shvybkzik?*" It was their father, Nicholas Romanov II, the former tsar. He liked to address Anastasia by her nickname "Shvybkzik," which was German for "Little Mischief." She thought he was beginning to believe in her powers now that Uncle Grigori could no longer take credit for Alexei's healing. Mother, though, firmly believed the holy man was still doing God's work from beyond the grave.

"Yes, Papa. He's doing much better now."

"Good," he said, although he still had a grim expression. These days spent at Ipatiev House, along with his loss of the people's support and all the good

Russians lost in the war, continued to weigh heavily on him.

Her father was five-foot-seven, with a strong build and a magnificent mustache/beard combination. He had a very regal disposition despite being dragged down from the throne by the Bolsheviks. But his eyes were probably his most distinguishing feature. The complete opposite of Uncle Grigori's, Nicholas II's Danish-given blue eyes were piercing and instantly instilled confidence in whoever he was talking to.

"Will we get to go home soon?" she asked.

"Yes, I'm sure we will. Just as soon as the Duma gets settled." The Duma was the provisional government set up by the Bolsheviks following the tsar's removal from power.

"They had no right to take the throne from you," she said. "God himself gave you the authority to rule."

"Perhaps God chose wrong. I've led so many of my people to their deaths. Many Russians have become destitute because of me."

She shook her head. "It wasn't your fault! Uncle Willy started the war."

His eyes seemed to stare at something very far away. "I should have listened to Grigori and kept us out of it. He urged me not to enter the war, and I wouldn't listen. I shouted that it wasn't his place to advise me on such matters."

He continued to stare off into space. At that moment, Mama entered. "How is he?" she asked, referring to Alexei.

Alexandra Feodorovna was of German ancestry, although only a fool would question her love for Russia. She maintained a regal countenance despite no longer being the empress consort.

"I am feeling better, Mama," Alexei said.

Alexandra knelt beside his bed and gave a smile that was rare these days. "Not even death can stop Our Friend from helping us in these dire times. God will see us through this, I have no doubt."

Anastasia desperately wished she had her mother's confidence, but things seemed to be getting worse all the time. There was something Papa wasn't telling them. She could see it on his face. Anastasia feared the situation was even worse than they were being led to believe.

Glava 3

Nelly parked the truck inside an abandoned barn in Moscow. She had just arrived in the city after driving all night. She had stopped seeing White Army aeroships after leaving Petrograd, so allowed herself a speck of hope she would have some breathing room for a while.

She grabbed a flashlight and exited the cab, still trembling. One moment, Sam had been there, and the next, he was dead. She had seen death before, but never like that. When she went on her first adventure as a kid, her friends had shielded her from the worst violence, but there was no one to protect her now.

Wood and detritus crunched beneath her feet as she rounded the truck toward the cab. Her breath was especially visible in the glow of the flashlight. An owl hooted somewhere nearby. *You're probably wiser than I was to come here.*

Nelly opened the trailer and went inside. She tried the lights and found them dead. The entire trailer was dead, including the Scribemeister, meaning she couldn't send a message back to New York. Must have been from the lightning strikes earlier, she decided.

A small cot lay across from the Scribemeister, and she sat down on it and began to weep softly. The tears flowed freely as she thought about Sam dying in front of her and how she might never see her family again. Her chest rose and fell with every sob.

Why had she taken this assignment? Oh, she knew well enough—the real question was, what sense did it make? She had gotten another person killed, a person she genuinely liked. Not that it mattered, of course; she would have felt guilty no matter who it was. She remembered the bandito Gnostagar in Pleroma whom she had refused to kill. That alone spoke volumes about her attitude toward sentient life. The phony Mexican had tried to kill her at a recreation of the Alamo, yet she had refused to give up her innocence.

In all the years that followed, she had managed to avoid bloodshed despite living in the wild new land of Oklahoma. Yet in the end, someone died because of her. And despite Sam's flirty attitude, he had a family of his own. The best-case scenario was Nelly returning home and delivering the news to his wife. The worst-case scenario? Nelly dying here and Sam's family never finding out what happened to him. At least in the best case, they would get closure.

She closed her eyes and took a series of deep breaths to regain her composure. She could have done this anytime, but she had needed to grieve for Sam. She now set her mind to getting out of this situation. She only had one hope of escaping Russia, and that meant getting to the town of Raivola. She suddenly realized she had driven in the opposite direction, as Raivola was about 37 miles northwest of Petrograd.

That compounded her other problem: She was low on fuel. She would need to go out and get some more, but she spoke hardly any Russian. Sam had been her translator, and while there was a Russian dictionary on top of the Scribemeister, her chances of posing as a native were slim to none.

Sighing, she got up and took the dictionary off the broken machine. She began looking up key phrases:

Privet. Hello.

Mne nuzhno toplivo. I need fuel.

U vas yest' dizel'noye toplivo? Do you have diesel fuel?

Gde zapravochnaya stantsiya? Where is the fuel station?

Skol'ko stoit vashe toplivo? How much does your fuel cost?

Skol'ko rubley? How many rubles?

Gde ya mogu kupit' yedu? Where can I buy food?

Spasibo. Thank you.

Do svidaniya. Goodbye.

There was also writing material in a drab metal desk next to the Scribemeister, so she wrote down the phrases on a sheet of paper. Tomorrow, she would go out in search of fuel.
Now, though...
Now, she would sleep.

* * *

Rough shaking woke Anastasia. One of the Red guards who had been keeping them prisoner at Ipatiev House stood over her. "Get up," he said harshly.
Her eyes swept over the rest of the room. Her family was also being awoken by other guards. Papa shouted at them to not be so rough with his children,

but one of the brutes slapped him hard enough to knock him down.

"Leave him alone!" Anastasia cried out.

"Shut up," the guard who had woken her said.

The family was ordered to get dressed. The children had sown their jewels into their garments at the behest of Alexandra when the parents' items had been confiscated by the guards. When they finished dressing, Yakov Yurovsky entered. He was a member of the Bolshevik secret police, the *Cheka*. He was an ugly man who had a forest of a beard adorning his face.

"What's going on?" Papa said.

Yurovsky explained, "The White Army is heading toward Yekaterinburg. The situation will be dangerous upon their arrival, and we anticipate violence will break out. For your own good, we are moving you to a safer location."

Anastasia groaned. All she wanted was to return home, but they would never get there at this rate.

The family, along with their servants, were then led to a small room in the sub-basement of the house and Alexei took a seat in a chair. Anastasia and her three sisters—Olga, Tatiana, and Maria—along with their father, stood idly against the wall next to it. The room smelled of dirt and mold, and the wallpaper was peeling off toward the floor.

Anastasia could not control her racing pulse, and she feared she would become physically ill by the overpowering anxiety this situation was forcing on her. She began to take deep, rapid breaths, and she found it increasingly difficult to get air into her lungs. Something wasn't right here. Why were they being made to wait in the sub-basement?

"I'm scared," she said.

"Everything will be fine," Papa said, but the lie couldn't have been more obvious.

Eventually, Yurovsky entered the room flanked by his guards. "Please let us depart already," Mama said. Anastasia couldn't help but notice her labored breathing as well.

Yurovsky ignored her. "You are all to be executed now."

"What?" Papa said. He turned to look at his family.

The guards raised their rifles and fired. The room lit up with muzzle flashes, and Anastasia's ears felt like they were exploding. Multiple bullets struck Papa in the chest, and he fell awkwardly to the ground. The rapport drowned out Anastasia's screams.

The guards then turned their guns on the rest of the family and servants. Alexei and Mama convulsed as the lead found its way home. Tatiana, Olga, and Maria fell next. Finally, the rounds slammed into Anastasia, propelling her backward headfirst into the wall with crushing force.

She knew no more.

* * *

Rasputin, sufficiently rested, headed to a nearby train station in Petrograd. However, he realized he didn't have any money on him. Normally, he could count on friends and admirers to loan him some rubles, but as he was believed to be dead—and most of the country now hated him—that made things decidedly difficult.

He, therefore, decided to return to his apartment at 64 on Gorokhovaya Street south of the Fontanka River in the middle of Petrograd.

He crept up to his apartment, being careful not to let anyone see his face, and put his key into the door. It did not open. *"Trakhni menya,"* he cursed softly. They must have changed the lock after his apparent death.

He decided to force his way in. He applied pressure to the knob, only to have it break off in his hand. He then leaned against the door, and it crashed inward like one of those paper Japanese ones. This puzzled him. *Was I always this strong?* If anything, he should have been weaker since his brush with death. He shrugged and attributed it to another one of God's blessings.

The apartment was empty, yet hopefully, the authorities had not discovered his hidden cache of money. He quickly made his way over to the middle of the floor, intending to be gone before the broken door was noticed. He pulled up the floorboard and smiled as he discovered the box of rubles was still there. He snatched it up and fled from the building into the night.

* * *

The news soon went out into all of Russia. One of the guards bragged to friends that he had been among the ones entrusted with the proud duty of executing the Romanovs. The royal family was dead.

Among the first to be notified was Kornilov. He sat in his cabin trying to figure out what he was going to tell the Prokrovitel. The latter would most certainly pull all support from the White Army upon learning the news.

He must have sat there for an hour mulling over different ways to phrase what he must say. Eventually, he ran out of time as the holo-projector lit up and the distorted silhouette of the Prokrovitel appeared. "I know what you're going to say."

"I..." His mouth was dry, and he felt the need to repeatedly lick his lips. "I am sorry. I thought we had more time."

"You are mistaken, General. We *do* have time, though it is still running out."

He straightened up in his chair. "But Anastasia Romanov is dead. She was executed along with her family last night."

But the Prokrovitel replied, "Must I repeat myself? We still have time. The former grand duchess is still alive. Though, once Lenin discovers that fact, he will move swiftly to rectify the situation."

"How can you possibly know that?" Kornilov said incredulously.

"Surely, General, you don't doubt the technology my company possesses? We have worked miracles time and again throughout the past few decades. Electricity, once a crude and dangerous invention, is now as common as sand. And it can do more than you could ever imagine."

He sighed. "Very well. Does this mean you will continue to support us?"

"Yes, General," the tinny, androgenous voice said. "Assuming you secure Anastasia Romanov before it is too late."

He took a deep breath. "It shall be done."

"At the moment, she is not moving. But once she does, I will keep you abreast of her direction."

There was only one thing he could say to that. "Understood."

The holo-projector powered down. A still-nervous Kornilov pressed one of the many buttons on the desk. The voice of his lieutenant then came through a speaker on the wall. "Sir?"

"Tell the rest of our men our plans remain unchanged. We are to secure Anastasia Romanov at all costs."

"But, sir, she is dead."

"New intelligence suggests otherwise," he said, not wanting to reveal more about the Prokrovitel than was necessary.

"Understood, General. Request permission to keep this on a need-to-know basis. We don't want Lenin to suspect that we know."

Kornilov nodded. "Good idea, Lieutenant. Let's keep this close to our chests."

* * *

She slowly opened her eyes to a blinding headache and nausea. Her chest ached. The stench was overpowering. Where on Earth could she be?

There was darkness at first, and she found herself pinned down by a heavy weight. Struggling to move, she concluded a large sack of potatoes lay on top of her. With great effort, she managed to push herself up, and then she saw what it was.

Anastasia Romanov put a hand over her mouth to stifle the exploding scream. The bodies of her family and servants lay under her, and they had all been piled up in the back of a military truck. Alexei lay under her, his eyes still wide in shock. Papa was the one she had pushed off her, while her sisters were propped up against the walls of the truck. And underneath Alexei were the rest of the bodies stacked in multiple layers.

As a pampered royal, Anastasia had never experienced much misfortune in her life. Now, all the tragedy she had managed to avoid had caught up to her with interest. She began sobbing uncontrollably and taking breaths too fast for her lungs to keep up. She couldn't breathe, and she had to force her body to calm down.

Her powers. Maybe they could still save her family. With that in mind, she put her hands over Alexei and infused him with the healing energy that had saved him so many times before. She tried this for several agonizing minutes before giving up. Her brother didn't respond in the slightest. He was gone.

Everyone was dead. Everyone was dead.
Everyone was dead. Everyone was dead.
Everyone was dead. Everyone was dead.
Everyone was dead. Everyone was dead.
Everyone was dead. Everyone was dead.
Everyone was dead. Everyone was dead.

These thoughts consumed her mind whole. Everyone was dead. But why wasn't she among them?

The answer came to her when she sat up straight on the grisly mountain. Something clinked around in her shirt. She pulled it up and pieces of jewels fell out. She realized the valuables she had sewn into her clothing had saved her from the barrage of bullets.

But other members of her family had done the same thing, so why hadn't they been spared? Looking closer, she saw stab wounds in her sisters. They must have been bayonetted.

Her sobbing intensified. It only ceased when she heard voices coming closer. The truck swayed slightly as someone got in the front. Panic set in; if the soldiers found out she was alive, they would surely finish the job. She needed to escape before that happened.

Within minutes, the truck started up and pulled out. She desperately wanted to avoid finding out its destination, so she climbed over the bodies in her path toward the rear door. By this point, she was completely soaked in their blood, a fact that threatened to destroy her mind. Mentally speaking, she hung on by the slimmest thread.

When she made it to the door, she now knelt on the body of her mother. Anastasia shook her head to try and concentrate on the task at hand—and not on the anguished eyes of Mama. She tried the door handle but couldn't turn it because her hands were slick with the life essence of her family.

She applied both hands and managed to turn it. The door opened, but as she was on unsteady footing, she immediately lost her balance and fell out. She met the ground and hissed when her arms and legs scraped the hard gravel. She rolled along for about twenty feet, soaking up dirt and dust.

When she finally came to a stop, she didn't immediately stand back up. She wanted to be as small as possible in case the men in the truck turned to look back. Eventually, the vehicle turned and drove out of sight. When it did, she gingerly stood up.

She looked around. To her left through the trees, she spied the bank of an unfamiliar river—probably the Iset. To her right were more trees, and the scene resembled a country lane. She didn't know if she was still in Yekaterinburg since she wasn't overly familiar with the city.

Which way should she go now? She hesitated to follow the path the truck had taken in case it stopped up ahead or came back for her. Then again, there could be more trucks coming up behind her. With both options equally disheartening, she instead turned right and headed into the trees. Perhaps she could hide out in the woods for a while.

She suddenly realized she still wore her clothes from last night—her now-blood-soaked clothes. In addition, a ghastly stench emanated from them. She decided to try and clean herself off in the river when she got a chance.

In the meantime, she sat down against a tree and embraced the tears. This time, she wailed, not feeling the need to hold back anymore.

Papa had been chosen by God to rule Russia, hadn't he? Then, where was God last night? The Devil now controlled Russia, she decided. The vivid images of her slain family members, their eyes sharp with terror and surprise, flashed repeatedly through her fractured mind.

Eventually, her eyes ran dry, though her sobs continued. What was she to do now? Her beloved family was gone, along with the brave servants who had stayed despite the danger.

It was all that monster Yurovsky's fault. She feverishly wished more than anything she could make him feel the same agony she did. But how could she? He had an army behind him, and she was just one scared girl. To strike back, she would need a military of her own. But the Russian army was not an option.

Think, Anastasia. You still have powerful connections across Europe. Who can help you? There was Cousin Willy, but Papa had tried so hard to crush him during the war that she didn't think he would be willing to help.

There were dozens of Romanovs in Russia as of last night. Surely some of them survived. Only a handful—albeit the most important handful—had met their fate at Ipatiev House. She needed to know who was left that could help her.

Fortunately, she was not entirely without financial resources. She still had the jewels sewn into her clothes. She could trade those for whatever she needed, provided she found someone who wouldn't ask questions.

Her eyes became heavy and started drooping. She needed sleep but feared getting it out in the open where Yurovsky's dogs might find her. With difficulty, she rose and began wandering through the woods looking for a hiding place. Her chest still ached from being shot, and she continued to take labored breaths. This, combined with her exhaustion, caused her to stumble frequently as she sought sanctuary.

Glava 4

The Kremlin, Moscow.

Vladimir Lenin paced around his office. He was sweating in his suit yet too dignified to show it. The Premier of the new Soviet Union was troubled.

Of course, as it was February, the sweat was due to something else. Somehow, the Whites had taken Petrograd and disabled all their Tesla Towers. His engineers assured him the towers would resume normal operations within a few days, but in that time the Whites could wreak considerable havoc.

When Lenin had been informed of the White Army's dual triumph, he had acted swiftly and decisively. He knew full well Kornilov would make haste toward Yekaterinburg to secure the Romanovs for his purposes. Thus, the leader of the Red Army ordered the family's immediate execution.

And while they had confirmed the deaths of everyone at Ipatiev House, Lenin had a nagging feeling in the back of his mind. If even one Romanov escaped, it would be a colossal embarrassment for the Bolsheviks.

The knocking at the door pulled him from his thoughts. "Come in."

Lenin's second-in-command, Lev Bronstein—more commonly known as Leon Trotsky—entered the room. He, too, had been sweating. The Ukrainian-born revolutionary had attempted a failed revolution in 1905 and was banished to Siberia, but Lenin's rise to power ultimately enabled Trotsky's return. Now, the five-foot-nine Marxist served Lenin faithfully. "Good afternoon, *Lider!*"

"What have you got?" Lenin asked him as they stood face to face.

Trotsky kept his hands clasped behind his back in a formal stance. His face betrayed no emotion. "Yurovsky has confirmed the disposal of the Romanovs and their servants at Ipatiev House."

"Very good," Lenin said. "But we've known each other a long time, my friend. I know when you're holding information from me. So, tell me... what has gone wrong?"

Trotsky exhaled and brought his hands to his sides. "The body of Anastasia went missing from the truck that was carrying the corpses. The door was open when the men stopped at the mine they were to bury the bodies in. Yurovsky assures me the door opened by accident and the corpse fell out."

Lenin was not amused. "Surely, they retraced their steps and found the body where it fell, correct?"

Trotsky exhaled again. "They did retrace their steps, but they did not find young Anastasia."

Lenin calmly turned around, walked over to his desk, and shoved everything off it in a blind fury. "Yurovsky, that idiot! I should not have given him that prestigious assignment." He stormed back to Trotsky who had not moved and raised his index finger. "You tell him he is to find her and finish the execution before anyone discovers our blunder. If he fails, he will take her place in the mine."

"Understood!"

Lenin managed to calm himself. "Was there anything else?"

"Yes, Lider. Our engineer corps promises to have the Tesla Towers back online within 48 hours."

Lenin grit his teeth as he considered the situation. "Kornilov could cross the entire continent in that time. I want a Bone Smasher X to go after Anastasia."

"Sir, that will tear up large portions of the ground underneath Russia."

"I don't care. Do it."

"As you command, Lider. I will assign *Kapitan* Stalin to lead the operation."

"Stalin?" Lenin said. "He's a bit young, isn't he?"

"Yes, Lider, but he is very capable. I trust him with my life."

Lenin nodded. "Very well. Tell him to mobilize the fleet at once."

"At once, Lider!"

* * *

"Hello," Anastasia said. She couldn't stop fidgeting and her eyes darted rapidly to every conceivable space.

The rail-thin stall operator glanced at her before going back to his newspaper. "Take a look around, but don't loiter."

She was at a merchant's outdoor stall in Yekaterinburg. She hardly needed to be told to hurry; every moment she stayed out in the open she risked being spotted by Yurovsky's cold-blooded killers. "Just a newspaper, please." She reached to his left and grabbed one off a stack.

"That'll be 500 rubles," he said.

She had none. Thankfully, she had something even better. She reached into the inner lining of her dress and fetched a diamond-encrusted ruby. "I trust this will suffice?"

His eyes bulged from their sockets when he saw what she offered. He quickly snatched it and stared in profound amazement. Convinced he was satisfied with the trade, she pumped her legs to flee from the scene as soon as possible with the newspaper in tow.

Anastasia returned to her hiding spot among a tight grouping of trees with heavy foliage forming a convenient wall. She sat down and began reading the newspaper, trying not to cry again as she absorbed the gruesome details she had witnessed firsthand.

Toward the end of the article, she found the information she needed. Her grandmother, Maria Feodorovna—Papa's mother—had escaped to London with the other surviving Romanovs. Her heart lifted somewhat at this news. Unfortunately, Anastasia herself was still thousands of kilometers deep into enemy territory. She needed to get to London and rejoin what remained of her family.

The Red Army controlled all air travel between here and Petrograd, so her only option was to go by train. That necessitated another trade using her jewels, and thus she must involve at least one more person who might report her to Yurovsky.

She spent the next hour mulling it over. Eventually, she concluded she had no choice under the circumstances. During her extensive studies as a royal, she had learned of a Danish Theologian named Søren Kierkegaard who proposed what would eventually be called a leap of faith. Her only option now was to take the risk.

She quietly said a prayer to keep her safe.

* * *

It took Nelly the better part of a day to work up the courage to venture into Moscow in search of diesel fuel. She couldn't help but imagine every Russian she saw was eyeing her with suspicion, and she kept from speaking unless necessary.

Eventually, she found a fuel station that night. All she had was a small plastic container to store it in, and since the truck took many times the amount it could hold, she would need to make numerous trips, assuming she could get diesel in the first place.

She approached one of the pumps and tried to work out how to operate it. The instructions were, naturally, in Russian.

A tall, slim woman wearing a grease-covered jumpsuit came over to her. *"YA mogu vam pomoch'?"*

"Um..." Nelly signaled to wait a moment while she opened her dictionary. The attendant had said, "Can I help you?"

"Ah," Nelly said. "Da. U vas yest' dizel'noye toplivo?"

The attendant raised an eyebrow. "American?"

"Uh..." How should she answer? "Maybe."

"Your pronunciation is terrible," the attendant said. "What are you doing in Moscow?"

Nelly sighed. "I'm a journalist. I was reporting on the civil strife your country is experiencing. My partner got killed in the White Army attack at Petrograd."

The attendant looked astonished. "You were in Petrograd? And you made it out alive?"

"Sadly, only I made it out."

"Mne zhal'," the woman said. "I'm sorry."

"Thank you. And believe me, I know I'm not welcome here, and I would love to go home, but I need diesel fuel to power my truck. If you could help me, I would be eternally grateful, Miss..."

"Zenaida," she said. "Zenaida Petrov."

Nelly smiled, feeling that she was getting somewhere here. "Nice to meet you, Zenaida."

"Let me get straight to the point, as you Americans say. We are forbidden from doing business with your kind under Red Army laws."

Nelly's heart sank and she felt like she had just lost all hope. "Oh. I see. I'm sorry to have bothered you."

She turned to walk away. But Zenaida said, "*Odin moment, pozhaluysta.* I can help you, but it cannot be a straightforward transaction. Give me the money to cover the payment for any diesel you take, and I'll enter it in the register as me buying it for myself. You would have to make a number of trips because I can't risk your vehicle being seen here, but you would get what you need. In return, I need you to check on someone in Petrograd for me."

Her spirits abruptly lifted, Nelly said, "Who would I be checking on?"

Zenaida explained, "My little sister Alyona is staying with family up there. I haven't heard from them since the Whites took over. If you could make sure they're all right and send a message back to me by Scribemeister at an address I'm about to give you, I would be, as you say, eternally grateful."

Nelly was literally about to jump for joy when she caught herself. Realizing other fuel station employees were watching, she quietly said, "Thank you so much."

Zenaida grinned. "Hopefully, I'll be thanking *you* very soon."

* * *

The next night.

Anastasia's original plan was to bribe a random citizen to buy her a train ticket to Moscow on the Trans-Siberian Railway, but when she spotted Red Army soldiers patrolling the trains, she realized she couldn't get away with posing as a normal passenger.

Therefore, she decided to sneak aboard one of them. She took a risk by asking a stranger which one was headed to Moscow. Once she had the information she needed, she set about becoming a stowaway. Fortunately, she had bought new clothes and couldn't be recognized as easily.

Her new plan consisted of anxiously skulking about the train station while waiting for an opening to sneak into the grain car. At first, many people were milling about, and she feared she wouldn't be able to succeed.

Eventually, though, the crowd thinned enough to where she managed to dart into the open door of the car. Once inside, she frantically searched for a hiding spot among the crates of grain. The car was tightly packed—in addition to being dark and cold—and she had to squeeze between crates to find a suitable one.

Each crate was also nailed shut which, combined with the claustrophobic nature of the car, caused her panic to spike and her heart rate to accelerate again. She began to tremble as she feared being discovered.

However, she soon found a crate that hadn't been fully nailed shut, and after some struggling, managed to pry it open just enough to climb into it. Once she was inside, she sunk to her waist into the grains.

Suddenly, voices alerted her to the fact someone was entering the car. She quickly shut the lid and said a silent prayer they wouldn't discover her.

Several heart-stopping moments followed as the train attendants inspected the crates. When they got to hers, she began hyperventilating again and had to put a hand to her mouth to stifle the sound. Unfortunately, this made it much harder to breathe, but she was determined to endure.

"What's this?" one of the men said.

"What's what?" the other said.

"This one hasn't been fully nailed shut."

At this point, Anastasia was approaching physical illness.

"It's fine, don't worry about it."

"All right, but you're taking responsibility if we get in trouble."

Eventually, the men left, and she released the biggest exhale in her life. She spent the next minute trying to get air into her lungs. The crate hadn't been designed for human habitation, so the air lacked abundance. She considered pushing the lid up slightly to get more oxygen but was terrified the men would come back at the exact moment she did that.

Within ten minutes, she managed to calm down and relax somewhat. It was maybe another half hour before the train lurched forward on its 2,000-kilometer journey to Moscow, its wheels clacking away.

From there... she didn't know. She hadn't thought that far ahead. The fact of the matter was she had spent her whole life as a pampered royal. She had received the best education—she knew several languages and was well-versed in geography and world affairs—but no one had ever taught her how to fend for herself or navigate a hostile country.

She only knew she had to get to London, but she was merely improvising as she went. She desperately needed help and would have even accepted it from Uncle Grigori. He had always been uncouth and lecherous, but Anastasia had felt genuinely bad after he died.

After an indeterminate amount of time passed in the darkness, she managed to fall asleep despite the uncomfortable situation.

* * *

Rasputin's train arrived in Moscow. From here, he would have to board another one bound further east, as the station he arrived at—Nikolayevsky—did not send trains to Yekaterinburg, although it could receive trains coming from that direction.

He left the train and wandered through the station where he noticed Red Army soldiers. He had only recently found out about them after reviving in the Neva. They were led by a cur named Lenin who had savagely betrayed Rasputin's good friends the Romanovs. Well, Grigori Rasputin would right those wrongs by saving the royal family. With God watching over him, no harm would come to any Romanov.

He stopped. Being submerged in the Neva must have rejuvenated his nose because every smell now came in sharper and more defined. Not only that, but he noted an overall revitalization throughout his body.

"Hey, mister! Buy a paper?" A street urchin had appeared by his side carrying a satchel full of newspapers.

"Why, certainly, *mal'chik!* There weren't any papers on the train, so I don't know what has happened since I left Petrograd."

"Very exciting news, sir! You won't be disappointed."

Rasputin handed him a few rubles and took the paper. The urchin then set off in search of more customers. Rasputin didn't even open the paper—the front page told him all he needed to know.

He dropped to his knees in anguish. The Romanovs—executed!? It could not be! As he read the heartbreaking words, his heart became heavier than it had ever been. The urchin's cruel words echoed in his mind: *You won't be disappointed.*

People stopped to stare at the unkempt man with wild hair slumped on the floor. He didn't care. All was lost now. He had been far too late. He did the only thing he could think of now: He craned his head toward the ceiling and began talking to God. "Why? You have always been there for us! Why would you allow this to happen?"

He began sobbing. God had seen fit to save him but not his dear friends? It didn't make any sense. He knew full well he was a sinner while the Romanovs were good, so why save him instead? His thoughts were consumed with images of Nikolas and Alexandra, and more so their children Alexei, Olga, Tatiana, Maria, and Anastasia.

Where was the justice in any of this?

Glava 5

The *Belyy Terror* (docked at the Winter Palace). Kornilov was on the bridge of his aeroship when he received a Code 14: a call from the Prokrovitel. He immediately returned to his cabin to receive it.

He sat down in his chair and pushed the button to accept the call. The familiar distorted outline of a human face appeared. "Anastasia Romanov is on the move. She has boarded a train bound for Moscow. Get there at once and intercept her when she arrives."

"Understood," Kornilov said.

"Be careful," the Prokrovitel said. "Another one has just arrived in Moscow. I don't know who it is, but they are registering as an Awakened. Use all necessary precautions when you arrive."

"Couldn't we just capture that one and forget about Anastasia?"

"No. Their powers are unknown. You may secure them for my research if you feel so inclined, but Anastasia takes priority. I will be arriving tomorrow, so notify your subordinates I am not to be detained or otherwise kept waiting."

His patron ended the call, and Kornilov sat there in silence pondering their words. The Prokrovitel had only mentioned the Awakened a few times and only briefly. Supposedly, they were people with higher abilities that transcended human limitations. The Prokrovitel had been studying them for years, though Kornilov didn't know why they wanted Anastasia Romanov in particular.

It was rumored the youngest grand duchess could heal her ailing brother, but others had attributed that to Grigori Rasputin. Whatever the case, Rasputin was dead.

Kornilov returned to the bridge. "Mobilize the fleet! We're going to Moscow."

"That will take some time, General," his assistant commander said. "We're still repairing the damage we suffered just taking Petrograd."

Kornilov replied, "Then I suggest you hurry. The Prokrovitel is coming, and we can't keep them waiting."

"General, please. Do we really need the help of an outsider? We should be free to do what's best for Russia."

"We *are* doing what's best for Russia. Those Red Army savages will destroy this country if we don't stop them. Look at what they just did to the former tsar and his family. They cannot be allowed to control our motherland. Like it or not, we need the Prokrovitel's financial and technological help to overcome the might of Lenin's dogs."

The assistant commander sighed. "Very well. If that is what you feel is best, I will remain silent on the matter."

Kornilov put a reassuring hand on his shoulder. "Thank you. These are difficult times, but we shall get through them and lead Russia into the future."

The assistant commander nodded. "I will assign double shifts. We shall work the men to the bone, but they will be happy to be of service to Mother Russia."

* * *

Anastasia groggily opened her eyes. She had been in the dark crate for what seemed like an eternity, only getting out here and there to relieve herself in the far back of the train car. She had been subsisting on grains for sustenance, and when it had rained, she had stuck her head out the window and let it fall into her mouth.

"Now arriving at Nikolayevsky Station!" a distant voice said. Nikolayevsky was in Moscow. She had arrived! Now, it was simply a matter of getting off the train undetected.

She climbed out of the crate and fell to the floor, her legs weak after enduring the conditions of the past few days. She managed to get to her feet, however, and began pondering her escape plan.

Suddenly, voices sounded outside. Worse, some of them were coming closer. The door to the car began shaking as someone worked to get it open.

Anastasia ran to the back of the car in a frenzy before a pair of men entered. She attempted to hide among the maze of crates. The men kept coming closer, however.

"Something stinks in here," one of them said.

"I think it's coming from the back." Which was where she was hiding. She chastised herself; she should have done her business somewhere more discrete, but she hadn't thought to.

Now, the voices were on the other side of a crate next to her. She put her hands to her mouth to muffle her heavy breathing. One of the men shone a flashlight over the crate, but as she was crouched as far to the ground as she could physically get, he didn't see her.

"Looks like we might have a stowaway."

"I'll go report this."

No! She would be discovered if they thoroughly searched the car. It was a miracle she hadn't been spotted already.

One of the men opened another door opposite her and the crate. She hadn't realized it was there. Acting on impulse she exploded from her spot and pushed him out of the car before jumping out herself.

"Stop her!" one of them said.

She was now in a train yard behind the station. She pumped her legs better than any Olympic runner and blasted across the tracks. Her train had stopped on the outermost track, and she had to pass a dozen more before she got anywhere.

"Stop! Stop at once!" No way was that happening, not when Yurovsky's cold-blooded killers could be anywhere.

Up ahead, another train was coming in from the right. She decided to risk it and kept going. It blared at her as it advanced down the track.

"Stop! You'll be killed!" *Yes, I will... if I let you catch me.*

As she ran toward the track where the other train was coming at her, she briefly considered stopping because she wasn't sure if she would make it. Inwardly, she shook her head. She couldn't survive without taking risks.

Anastasia Romanov reached the track.

The train reached Anastasia.

Anastasia cleared the track the tiniest fraction of a second before the train sped past her. She felt the burst of wind from the sheer weight of something that heavy lumbering through. She had now put the train between her and her pursuers.

After crossing a few more tracks, she came to the terminal building. Spotting an open door in the back, she hurried in, closed it, and locked it. She was now in a rear corridor with offices. She made her way through the winding hallways and eventually arrived in the public area of the building.

She planned to shake off any pursuers by blending in with the crowd. With that in mind, she began walking casually while willing her frayed nerves to cooperate. She had been here before—her family had owned multiple private trains—and so she knew her way around. Once she reached the front, she could escape into Moscow.

After that, she still didn't know what she would do. She originally intended to find a train here that would take her west toward England, but now that she had been discovered, she needed to get out of here.

"You there! Halt!" She froze. A Red Army soldier a dozen meters away to the right was coming toward her. She abandoned all attempts to control her anxiety and bolted through the station, shoving anyone who got in her way. Plenty of people cursed her and gave her angry looks, but her feelings were the least of her concerns.

* * *

Rasputin sulked against the wall of the railway station in a semi-drunken stupor. He had been there for some time wallowing in his misery. His only consolation was no one had hassled him so far.

Suddenly, a girl ran past him. Looking up, he was astonished to see the face of young Anastasia. *I must be drunker than I thought.* Alcohol was being especially cruel tonight, he thought before going back to his bottle of vodka.

However, some Red Army curs also ran past him in the same direction the fake Anastasia had gone. "It's Anastasia Romanov! Don't let her get away!" one shouted in Russian.

Shocked, Rasputin realized there was more than booze at play here. Seeing a girl who resembled the youngest grand duchess was one thing, but here were men loudly proclaiming that had been her running by.

He scrambled to his feet and a feeling of lightheadedness came over him. He had been sitting on the floor longer than he realized. Within moments, the feeling passed, and he set off to join the chase. He needed to get to Anastasia before those mongrels did. If she had survived, perhaps God had not abandoned them after all.

Thankfully, he was still relatively fit from walking across the country on his various pilgrimages. Within moments, he had built up incredible speed and was effortlessly bowling people over in his one-man stampede.

The holy man soon caught up with the bastards who were chasing Anastasia. He grabbed both by the backs of their uniforms. "You leave her alone!" he said in Russian before slamming their heads together.

They crumpled to the floor, and he grabbed one of their rifles. These two may have been dealt with, but there would surely be more.

He needed to catch up with Anastasia and get her somewhere safe.

* * *

"You leave her alone!" someone yelled behind her. The voice sounded familiar, but Anastasia couldn't stop to look back. She kept running and soon burst through the station entrance.

She ran across the street—nearly getting hit by angry motorists—and down an alley before collapsing to the ground. Her lungs were on fire, and she could barely breathe. She knew she couldn't waste time here, but her body demanded rest. So, she sat there against a fence, her mouth open gasping for air. Her stomach churned and roiled, and if she tried to get back up, she would probably empty partially digested grains all over the ground.

She needed to get some real food when she recovered.

She stayed there for a while, probably far longer than she should have. Finally, she felt well enough to get back up. She then wandered through Moscow for hours, trying to find food and shelter. But she kept getting spotted by Red Army troops and had to keep running, periodically stopping to rest.

Ultimately, she came to a wooded area where she found an old barn. Inside, there was a truck with a trailer attached. Thinking this could be a good hiding spot, she slipped inside. She fumbled for the light switch, finding it after a few minutes. However, nothing happened when she flipped it.

Undeterred, she continued to feel about in the darkness until her hand landed on a cylindrical object. A flashlight! She turned it on and surveyed the trailer. The interior consisted of multiple pieces of equipment as well as a cot and something bundled in a coat in the corner. Good, she could rest.

But before she did that, she noticed there was a Scribemeister along the wall. Perhaps she could send a message to her grandmother. Unfortunately, those hopes were dashed when she discovered the machine didn't work. She sighed. *Of course it's not working. Nothing in my life is working now.*

Or so she thought. But then a small cooler on the other side of the trailer caught her attention. Curious, she opened it and found food inside. *Finally! Something good happened.*

Anastasia Romanov had a decent meal for the first time since her ordeal at Ipatiev House.

* * *

Rasputin had literally picked up Anastasia's scent and tracked it to a nearby alley. No doubt about it; she had been here. But where had she gone? Her scent had diminished too much to follow reliably.

Strangely, his eyes blurred for a moment before his vision returned with greater clarity than ever before. Now, he could make out the minuscule outline of footprints along the ground. They were far too small to be his, so they must have been Anastasia's.

He followed them, finding that they grew brighter the farther he went. He reasoned the closer he got to Anastasia, the fresher her tracks became.

He was back on the trail, but what were these strange changes coming over his body? He could only conclude God was continuing to give him more divine assistance.

* * *

Nelly returned to the barn with the last container of fuel she needed to make the trip back north. With any luck, she would be able to return home soon.

She went inside the trailer and groped for the flashlight. However, it was not in the same spot she left it. Annoyed, she decided to just go to bed—or cot, as it were.

She sat down on the cot, only to find something was already on it. There was a scream and Nelly shot up, confused as hell. Someone was in here with her.

The mystery person knew where the flashlight was because they quickly grabbed it and turned it on, revealing an impossible face. "Don't touch me!" the girl yelled.

Nelly couldn't believe it. "You're Anastasia Romanov!"

"So, what!" Anastasia said. There was a long pause as the grand duchess studied Nelly. "You don't look like one of Yurovsky's killers."

Nelly replied, "No, I'm not with the Red Army. I'm not with *any* army. My name is Nelly Flowers and I'm a reporter from America. I was covering your country's turmoil when my partner and I were attacked by White Army forces at Petrograd. He was killed. His body's actually right over there. I guess you didn't see it."

Another long pause. Finally, "Okay, Nelly Flowers. I appreciate your honesty."

"If you don't mind my asking," Nelly said, "your family... are they really...?"

Anastasia's expression said it all. If a face could be capable of crumbling in agony, then the former grand duchess' most certainly did. "I'm sorry! I shouldn't have asked."

"They were...!" Anastasia started before a sob choked up her. "I can still see them. That monster Yurovsky told us we were to be executed so casually as if it didn't mean a thing to him. Then they started shooting, bullets slamming into them, blood spurting everywhere..." She was staring ahead, but not at Nelly. Anastasia Romanov was trapped in a nightmare she could not wake from.

Nelly reached out and took hold of the 17-year-old's shoulders. "Look at me. Focus on *me*. You're safe here. No one's going to hurt you." It was an audacious statement considering they could be attacked at any time and Nelly had no weapons, but she had to say *something* comforting.

Anastasia's eyes locked onto Nelly's. "Nelly Flowers." It was a declaration.

Nelly nodded. "Yes."

"Okay. I'm calm now. But if I don't have something to distract me, I inevitably think about *it*."

"Okay," Nelly said. "I just brought back the last of the fuel I need to get away from here. Come on, we can finish filling up the tank together."

"All right," Anastasia said timidly.

They went outside, Nelly holding the gas can and Anastasia holding the flashlight. Nelly directed them to the right side of the truck. "Hold the light on the gas cap there."

The former grand duchess did so, and Nelly proceeded to twist the cap, quickly removing it. Nelly then turned the gas can upside down and poured the diesel. There was a *glug-glug-glug* as gravity worked its magic. Within moments, it was done.

"They would never let us do things like this at Tsarkoye Selo. They said a royal must not do such things."

"I'm sure you had people to do that for you," Nelly replied.

"Yes, we had many servants. Until the Bolsheviks forced Papa to abdicate, and we were sent to Ipatiev House. Only a few remained at that point."

They went back inside the trailer where Anastasia told Nelly everything that had happened to her up until she had found the trailer.

"I'm so sorry for everything you've been put through," Nelly said.

"Thank you, Nelly. That is a beautiful name, by the way."

Nelly smiled. "My parents certainly thought so. But what will you do now?"

Anastasia began pacing back and forth across the trailer's interior. "I need to get to London to join what remains of my family. My grandmother, Maria Feodorovna, will know what to do after that."

"All right," Nelly said. "I was about to go to see some old friends of mine. They have an aeroship, so they can help you get out of Russia."

Anastasia stopped pacing and her eyes lit up. "Really? You would help a stranger like me?"

Nelly chuckled. "Seeing as how most of the country knows you, you're hardly a stranger."

"I suppose that's true."

"I was going anyway. You might as well come with me. I need to get out of Russia myself."

"These friends of yours," Anastasia said. "Do you trust them?"

Nelly beamed. "With my life!"

There was a pause. Then, Anastasia said, "Okay. I'll go with you. I can't do enough to properly express my gratitude but thank you. Oh! I know." She reached into her pocket and produced the single most amazing jewel Nelly had ever seen. It was a blue gem studded with diamonds.

"Holy Okmulgee!" Nelly said, slipping back into her Oklahoma accent.

Anastasia looked puzzled. "What is 'Ok-mul-gee'?"

"Oh. Nothing. It's just an expression I picked up as a kid. But are you really giving me that?"

"Yes. I still have plenty left. We may need to use more of them before our journey is finished."

"Okay!" Nelly said happily, taking the quite possibly priceless item. "Thank you. I don't plan on selling this; I just want it so I can prove I met Anastasia Romanov."

"You can do whatever you want. You have provided me sanctuary in your quaint vehicle. It's the least I can do."

For being the least she could do, it was a hell of a lot. Maybe priceless diamond-studded gems were commonplace in the grand duchess' life, but Nelly knew people back in Oklahoma who would've been set for life with one of these.

"All right!" Nelly said. "I'll fire up the truck and drive us out of here. You can stay here in the trailer. Just keep your head down in case anyone decides to peek through the window."

"I just have one more question. Where exactly are these friends of yours?"

Nelly explained, "Their aeroship was last seen in Raivola. That's actually why I took this assignment. I was hoping to see them again after all this time."

"When was the last time you saw them?"

"1889."

"What?" Anastasia said, agape. "You haven't seen them since before I was born, and you expect them to help us?"

Nelly shrugged. "We share a deep bond that can't be broken by time. I believe in them."

Groaning, Anastasia said, "Fine. But I pray to God this works."

Nelly opened the door and hopped out. As she walked out of sight, she said, "God's a giant tree."

"What does that mean?"

Nelly smiled but said nothing more. Perhaps later she would regale Anastasia with the story of her first adventure.

* * *

Rasputin followed Anastasia's footprints to a barn in a wooded clearing. Inside, he found a truck with a trailer attached. He fervently hoped the grand duchess was inside one of these and well.

Her scent emanated strongly from the trailer. He crept around to the side of it and reached out to take hold of the door handle. But before he could grab it, the truck roared to life and lurched forward. He took hold of the back of the trailer, and they went off into the night.

Glava 6

Nelly started the engine and after a few moments, the truck came back to life.

They were soon on the main highway of Moscow. As long as they didn't get caught, they would arrive at Petrograd by dawn. Nelly's main concern was keeping Anastasia from being discovered while she checked on Zenaida's family.

Suddenly, familiar lights filled the night sky. It wasn't until they came closer that she saw they were Red Army aeroships. Fortunately, it didn't appear they were after her, as they were speeding across the city to the west. Where more aeroships were coming in from the opposite direction.

Wait... what?

The Red Army vessels began firing on the other group of aeroships. Nelly realized the others must be White Army. The sky quickly erupted into a fireworks show of lightning and fiery explosions. *Not again!* Should she speed up? She feared doing so would call attention to the two women.

Debris began falling onto the streets, causing the other cars on the road to swerve, hitting either the median, the outer rails, or one another, resulting in the scream of grinding metal. Nelly employed some quick maneuvers to keep from getting smashed between two vehicles. Left; right; speed up; slow down; her deft steering kept them intact. The renowned musician Nelly Flowers conducted a symphony with the vehicle's controls.

She barely registered something falling off the back of the trailer.

She pressed the intercom button on the dashboard. "Hang on, things just got crazy!" She then remembered the trailer had no power, so Anastasia was on her own back there.

Without warning, one of the White Army aeroships broke from its formation and made a beeline toward the highway. Nelly desperately hoped it wasn't coming for *them.*

Those hopes were seemingly dashed when the vessel landed on the road in front of her blocking all lanes. She slammed on the brakes and the truck careened to a stop in front of the aeroship. White Army troops then disembarked from it, rifles in hand and pointed squarely at the truck.

Nelly put it in reverse and tried to back up, only to crash into another car behind them. The soldiers sprinted over and aimed their guns at Nelly. "Get out of the vehicle now!" one of them yelled in English.

Now surrounded, she weighed her options. She could try charging forward, but she would quickly crash into the aeroship. No, her only option was to cooperate and hope they weren't after Anastasia.

She reached for the door handle to her left. "No sudden movements!" they said.

She opened the door at a snail's pace and put her hands up. She hopped down from the cab and her arms were immediately forced behind her back. Something snapped down on her wrists and that was it.

* * *

A nauseous Anastasia picked herself up off the ground after flying into the wall when Nelly slammed on the brakes. What was going on out there and why was Nelly driving like a mentally insane person?

She staggered about, still dizzy and with a sore arm. The door to the trailer then burst open and strange men entered. "Get on your knees!" one of them yelled in Russian. She tried to run but they blocked the only exit from the trailer. One of them grabbed her by the wrist and forced her to the floor before handcuffing her.

She was scared, but it could have been worse. These were White Army soldiers. They didn't work for Yurovsky. Many White Army soldiers had been loyal to Papa. She could only hope these men were, although the rough treatment gave her doubts.

"My name is Anastasia Romanov! I'm the grand duchess!" she said in Russian.

"We know who you are. You're the target."

She began to panic. The target? Then, she was to be killed after all? She struggled to break free, but these were strong men.

They dragged her outside where more were holding Nelly. "I'm sorry!" Nelly said, tears in her eyes.

Anastasia blurted out, "It's not your fault."

"Stay strong, Ana!" Nelly said.

She found she liked being called "Ana." She took comfort in the familiarity and made the decision then and there to keep her head high. She would not die confused and scared like her family. If she had to die, she would die smiling.

* * *

The two women were brought aboard the aeroship where they were made to sit against the wall of the cargo hold. The crew's commander, judging by the pips and medals on his white uniform, then entered from the opposite direction. "It really is you!" he declared upon seeing Ana who brightened up at his entrance.

"General Kornilov!" she said.

"In the flesh, as you say. I am glad you survived your ordeal. I am terribly sorry for what happened to the royal family. We tried to get there before that bastard Yurovsky carried out his vile act, but we were tragically unsuccessful."

"I take it you're Lavr G. Kornilov?" Nelly said.

"Yes?" he said, scrutinizing her. "And who are you?"

"A friend," Ana said. It felt good to be called a friend of royalty. "She gave me shelter while I was being pursued by the Red Army."

"Ah! In that case, you have my deepest gratitude."

Ana then said, "General, why are we being treated like criminals?"

It was only now that he realized they had been handcuffed. "What? Who did this?" A few of his soldiers, who had gathered around them, raised their hands. *"Derzost!* Free them at once."

The men complied, and the two women were allowed to stand up again. "Thank you, General, but you still haven't explained what you want with us," Nelly said.

"With you? Nothing. Our business is with the grand duchess. You see, we have been able to get this far only with the financial and technological support of a certain someone. Our benefactor supplied us with everything we need—on the condition we arrange a meeting between them and Anastasia."

"What does this person want with me?" Ana said.

Kornilov replied, "Better to let them explain for themselves."

I've got a bad feeling about this, Nelly thought. Still, maybe this was better than being caught by the Red Army. "General, I have a request."

"Yes, Miss...?"

"Flowers. Nelly Flowers. I would like safe passage out of Russia so I can return to my family."

"Certainly! You have been invaluable in your assistance to young Anastasia. I would be happy to ensure your safety in leaving our fine country."

"Thank you." It sounded good, but it wasn't over yet. They still had to meet this mysterious benefactor.

Nelly and Anastasia were given their own cabin aboard the *Belyy Terror* (the name certainly didn't sit well with Nelly, but she was in no position to complain). Anastasia marveled at the posh quarters. *"Très magnifique!* We each get out own bed."* Indeed, it was a fancy flying hotel room.

"How many languages do you speak?" Nelly said.

"I speak three well: English, Russian, and French. I was never particularly fond of our French tutor Monsieur Gilliard, but at least he taught us some useful information. My siblings and I were also learning German, but we had to stop because of Uncle Willy."

Nelly cocked an eyebrow. "Who's Uncle Willy?"

"Kaiser Wilhelm of Germany. He started the war, and after that happened, everything German became outlawed in Russia. People even suspected Mama of being a spy because she was German. The people were so ungrateful, it makes me sick."

Nelly sat down on the bed closest to the door. A large bay window presented a beautiful aerial view of Moscow while letting in abundant sunlight which warmed her whole being. "Tell me about your family.

What were they like? All I know is what I've heard and read."

Nelly sat down on the bed next to hers. "I'm very proud of them. Mama and my sisters Olga and Tatiana were nurses in the war, but Maria and I were too young, so they left us out. Boo!

"Mama's favorite color was mauve. Everything had to be mauve in her rooms. Mauve this, mauve that!

"Let's see... We had three precious dogs. Tatiana had Ortipo, a French bulldog. Alexei had a cocker spaniel named Joy. And I had Jimmy, the best Cavalier King Charles Spaniel ever.

"What are you smiling at?"

Nelly replied, "It's just that, you seem a lot more upbeat now. You were a wreck just a day ago, and now you're conversing with me like nothing happened."

Anastasia lowered her head. "It isn't that I'm not crushed by the loss of my family. But they wouldn't want me sulking. They would want me to stay strong."

"I'd say you're doing a very good job of that."

"Thank you."

* * *

The next morning, Nelly and Ana were brought back into the cargo hold. However, this time, no soldiers were around except for Kornilov. "Our benefactor has arrived."

Nelly tensed. This mystery person had better not try anything with Ana.

"Very well. Bring them in," Ana said.

A klaxon sounded, and the cargo bay doors began opening. Soon there appeared a cadre of people outside on the landing pad. At the center of the group was a bizarre-looking woman in a wheelchair. Her face was painted white, and her hair shot backward over her head as if she had recently been electrified. She was middle-aged, but as she looked so haggard, she would have passed for twenty years older than even that.

Her entourage consisted of obvious mercenaries. They wore armored vests and carried electro-rifles. They accompanied her as her electric wheelchair carried her into the cargo hold where she stopped a few yards from the three of them.

Kornilov said, "May I present—"

Nelly cut him off. "Victoria Grimfall!"

The woman in the wheelchair said, "How do you know my name?"

They had met before during Nelly's first adventure, but that was some three decades earlier. Dr. Grimfall had been that monster Garasheth's (AKA Robert Stone) scientist and built a machine to re-open the door to the Gnostagar world of Pleroma. She happily did this despite knowing the Gnostagar would invade Earth.

Or, at least, she *had*. But the timeline had changed so Nelly and Grimfall never met. Only Nelly and—presumably—Eva, Michael, and Jay had retained their memories of those events.

Time had not been kind to the poor geneticist. She was now severely emaciated and seemed to have trouble even moving her head. Also, her glasses threatened to fall off at any moment. Still, Nelly could never forget that face.

"That's difficult to explain," Nelly said.

"Hmmm," Grimfall said. "In 1889 I got the distinct impression I had forgotten something important. Was that something... meeting you?"

"Yes. Originally, my friends and I had been captured by Robert Stone and taken to your prison in Death Valley. You had constructed a portal to allow the Gnostagar to invade us. But one of my friends disrupted the machine and we were transported to Pleroma. Except for you. I think you were standing out of range."

"Yes," Grimfall rasped. "Was that in April?" Nelly nodded. "Fascinating. I remember building the portal generator, but then Robert Stone died mysteriously. I could never escape the feeling there was more to the story than what I could remember. At the time, Director Stone was in the process of bringing me the descendant of Jeanne de Fleur. I suppose you are her?"

"No, I thought I was at first, but it turned out I wasn't. Not that it matters now. We stopped Stone—or Garasheth as we knew him—and saved the world."

"Um... excuse me?" Ana said. She was anxiously looking back and forth between Nelly and Grimfall. "I'm sorry to interrupt, but I am very confused. What are you two talking about?"

Grimfall gave a hoarse chuckle. "My apologies, Anastasia Nikolaevna. I pushed General Kornilov to hurry and retrieve you, yet here I am wasting time. I find scientific problems to be delightfully irresistible, and this one had vexed me for three decades.

"Let us get back on track. Anastasia, I require your powers as an Awakened."

"Powers?" Nelly said. "What powers?"

Grimfall explained, "I have been seeking the powers incorrectly attributed to the starets, the Mad Monk, Grigori Rasputin. I have come to learn of certain people with extraordinary abilities. I call them the Awakened."

"Oh! You want me to ease your pain?"

"No, dammit! I'm dying. I've contracted amyotrophic lateral sclerosis. I need you to restore my health before it's too late."

Ana frowned. "I'm sorry; I'm not that strong. I can only ease suffering."

"Wait a minute!" Nelly said. Then, to Ana, "You have powers?"

"Yes. I've been using them to make my brother's hemophilia less severe."

Incredible! It's finally happening.

Grimfall was not amused. "What do you mean, you can only ease suffering?"

"I deeply apologize, but I can't reverse a person's condition."

The good doctor's eyes twitched. "Well. That's a problem, isn't it?"

All this time, Kornilov had looked hopelessly confused. "I don't understand half the things that have been said here, but if young Anastasia can't help you, does that mean you'll withdraw your support?"

"Silence!" Grimfall said. "I need to think for a minute. Let's see..."

"If I can isolate the source of the grand duchess' powers, I may be able to amplify them. But I'll need to run a battery of tests, and I don't know if I have time." She was sweating now.

Nelly decided to reveal what she knew. "I think I can shed some light on this. I believe I know where Ana's powers come from."

"You do? Out with it, and hurry!" Grimfall said.

Nelly explained, "When we were transported to Pleroma, we had to undergo a series of trials. As it turns out, Pleroma is the universal subconscious where all human thoughts and memories are stored."

Nelly considered how best to break it down. "Pleroma is basically a giant brain for all mankind. At least, that's how I understood it. Every human mind is connected to this bigger mind. The Gnostagar are living representatives of every human culture. I guess the best way to put it is, they're physical, sentient figments of our imaginations."

"I know that," Grimfall said testily. "They established diplomatic relations with the major nations of the world, but our relationship with them broke down sometime after. We could have gained so much if not for their selfishness."

"They wanted us to forge our own path free of excessive influence. With all they had done to us in the past, can you blame them for not wanting history to repeat itself? Besides, the future is always in flux, so anything they told us would be subject to change.

"Anyway, when we passed the trials, we were allowed to meet God—or something very close to it. This being took the form of a giant tree, and it explained that we had just unlocked the full potential of the human brain. It said it would take decades to achieve, but now it looks like it's begun."

Grimfall stared at her in wonder. "Fascinating! As a scientist, I don't believe in God. But I *do* believe in the god of human potential. Essentially, you're saying Anastasia's brain is the key to saving my life. Hmmmm, yes. But why stop at mine? If I could study her brain, I could cure every disease and affliction in the world. One sacrifice for the greater good."

All the color drained from Ana's face. "Sacrifice?"

Grimfall gave her the most subtle of nods. "Yes. To study your brain in the greatest detail, I will have to remove it."

"Now, wait just a minute!" Nelly said. "From what I understand, you're pretty advanced technologically. You are, after all, the one who built those crazy machines in the prison. Surely, you have something that can study Ana's brain through her skull."

But Grimfall said, "I do not. Our focus at Bronte-Astrape Enterprises was never the human body. It was electricity and its applications in weapons and defense. Yes, I could probably boost Anastasia's powers enough to heal myself, but if I can dissect her brain, I could heal *everyone*. I'm sorry, but that is the obvious path we must take."

Kornilov stepped forward to confront the doctor. "This is madness! I am a tsarist through and through, and I will not allow you to harm the only remaining member of the royal family."

Grimfall rolled her eyes—or as much as she could with the poor condition of her body. "I tire of your lack of vision, General. I am doing this for the greater good."

Pointing an accusing finger at her, Nelly said, "Since when did you ever care about the greater good? You were willing to let all of mankind be enslaved in the name of science!"

Grimfall explained, "I had hoped the Gnostagar would have much to teach us. But due to their repeated failures, I was forced to focus my efforts on humanity itself. I have made it my life's mission to advance science as much as possible. And with this opportunity alone, I will double the progress I made over the past three decades."

Kornilov withdrew his revolver from its holster and pointed it at Grimfall's head. "Enough! I was a fool to trust you. Be gone from this place before I am forced to clean *your* brain off the floor."

"Hmph. You not only lack vision but any intelligence at all. Otherwise, you would have noticed you're both outnumbered and outgunned in here." To her men, she said, "Take the former grand duchess into custody."

One of them stepped forward to comply. Kornilov pointed his gun at him, but the others raised their rifles and fired an arc of electricity at the general, electrocuting him in place. Kornilov spasmed uncontrollably and fell against the wall whereupon he slumped to the floor. During the attack, there had been very little sound other than a faint crackling. Kornilov's men in the back would not have heard anything.

Nelly got between Grimfall's mercs and Ana, holding her arms out as wide as possible. "Leave her alone!" They immediately tossed her aside and took Ana.

"Let me go!" Ana yelled in defiance as she struggled against her new captors.

Suddenly, the klaxon once again sounded, and a red light pulsated on the ceiling. Nelly followed Grimfall's gaze to Kornilov who had stood up and had his hand on a button embedded into the wall. He then collapsed again. Grimfall tried to issue orders, but her hoarse voice had no hope of being heard over the siren now screaming throughout the cargo hold.

The interior door behind Nelly opened and a squad of White Army soldiers charged into the room. The man holding Ana was put down with a bullet to the head. Nelly leaped and tackled her to the ground to get her out of the way of all the weapons now being discharged in the confined space. It was an unholy light show of dancing electricity and muzzle flashes.

Nelly took Ana by the hand and led her to a side door. Opening it, they found a ladder that led down to the landing pad, and they descended.

Nelly instructed Ana to go first while the former would do her best to serve as a human shield if necessary. While climbing down after her, Nelly kept her eyes locked on the door they had just exited. Her blood froze when one of Grimfall's mercs stuck his head out and pointed his electro-rifle at her. However, he abruptly shuddered and dropped his rifle—and himself—out of the aeroship when a bullet burst from his chest. He flew past the two women on his way to the landing pad where his body smashed against the otherwise pristine paint job.

Within minutes, Ana touched down followed by Nelly who grabbed the electro-rifle. The two of them went over to the side of the landing pad and examined their surroundings. They stood atop a tower built into the front of the Palace, and Palace Square lay across from them with Alexander Column in the center.

Ana, who used to live here, said, "Let's descend the tower and take refuge inside the Palace."

Nelly gazed over at Grimfall's black aeroship which sat on the other side of the pad. The doctor and her troops were exiting the ramp of the *Belyy Terror* and heading back to their own much bigger ship. Looking around the roof of the Palace, Nelly spied at least a dozen more of Grimfall's private fleet docked along various other landing pads all over the building. Conversely, there weren't nearly as many of Kornilov's ships around, and the General was no doubt in no position to lead his forces anyway.

"No," Nelly said. "Grimfall has enough firepower here to level the Palace and force Kornilov's men to surrender. We're not safe here. We need to continue the original plan and head for Raivola."

"What can your friends do that an entire army can't?"

"They can work miracles."

They descended the stairs to the ground. Nelly spotted a manhole cover on the ground and rushed over to open it.

"Do we actually have to go down there?" Ana said.

"Yes. They can easily follow us on ground level. We can lose them in the sewers."

Ana groaned but said nothing more. They were about to enter when the sound of a speeding vehicle cut through the air. What looked like her truck raced through Palace Square toward them. It swerved and came to a stop a few feet away.

Glava 7

The previous night.

Rasputin gingerly picked himself off the ground. He had fallen off during all the commotion due to the truck's crazy driver. He had hit the ground with incredible force and then he had been hit by another car sending him flying into yet another vehicle. Thankfully, his increased durability allowed him to walk away from that.

The scene all around him was chaos. Cars blocked the street, many of them having smashed into one another trying to avoid smashing themselves against the aeroship obstructing the road ahead. People yelled in confusion and fear, and many were injured.

Armed soldiers dragged Anastasia into the aeroship. Rasputin grit his teeth in anger, adrenaline surging through him. *You will not harm her!* He charged forward to the vessel which lay roughly 100 yards away.

He arrived swiftly, but by then everyone had gone inside and shut the doors. He pounded against the hull in rage, but it did no good. The vessel's engines came back online with a loud hum, and it rocketed into the sky with a northwest heading.

Recently, the White Army had taken the Winter Palace in Petrograd which lay in that direction. That must have been their destination.

He strode over to the truck Anastasia had been riding in and got in. There was enough fuel to reach Petrograd, so he could be thankful for that much at least. Finding the keys were still in the ignition, he started the engine and drove off after the White Army aeroship.

After driving all night, he arrived in Petrograd. He was annoyed to find a security checkpoint at the city's main entrance. But he had spent much time in Petrograd and knew all the back roads leading into the capital.

It took longer to sneak in, but he couldn't risk getting caught at the checkpoint. Eventually, though, he made it to the Winter Palace later that morning. Here, he faced another challenge. The Palace was surrounded by aeroships, any one of which Anastasia could be on. She could even have been in the Palace.

Rasputin took his hands off the steering wheel and balled them into fists. Time was of the essence, and for all he knew, he may already be too late.

He was debating what to do when the sound of gunfire erupted from the Palace. He needed to get in there! But it was difficult pinpointing exactly where the cacophony emanated from.

His newfound eagle-like vision locked onto Anastasia and another woman descending a landing pad tower in front of Palace Square. He immediately slammed onto the accelerator and drove across the wide, open area, scaring quite a few people in the process.

The holy man went as fast as he could for as long as he could. Eventually, he was forced to bring the truck to a halt in front of a wide-eyed Anastasia and the mystery woman.

* * *

"Why is your truck here?" Ana said. "And who's driving it?"

"Those are very good questions," Nelly replied, electro-rifle pointed at the cab.

They didn't have to wait long for answers. Out stepped the most pitiful-looking man Nelly had ever seen. He had long, wild hair and a matching beard, while his clothes looked filthy. His stench was almost overpowering to boot.

But without a doubt, his most distinctive feature was his eyes. They were focused to an insane degree, almost as if they stared into the future.

He focused his attention on Ana and began speaking to her in an excited tone.

Ana gaped at him. *"Dyadya Grigoriy!"*

"Do you know this man?" Nelly said.

"Um..." Ana was at a loss for words. "Yes. He is our family's friend Uncle Grigori. But he's supposed to be dead."

Grigori motioned for them to get in the truck. Nelly hopped in the driver's seat, followed by Ana and the new arrival. Nelly turned the vehicle ninety degrees and sped away from the scene.

As they raced through Petrograd, Nelly said to Grigori, "Do you speak English?"

He said something in Russian.

"No, he doesn't," Ana said. "He's a peasant so he hasn't had access to advanced learning as I have."

"Well, then, ask him what he's doing here and why he had my truck."

Nelly and Grigori began conversing in Russian. This went on for some time. Finally, Ana explained to Nelly all that Grigori had gone through since his attempted murder.

"Wow," Nelly said. "That's quite a story. He must be another Awakened, although his abilities seem to be more physical. Tell him 'Thanks' for bringing my truck back to me."

She did and he replied.

"He says 'It was my pleasure.'"

* * *

Grimfall and her troops reconvened on her secondary aeroship, the *Quandary*. There was a special stadium platform on board the bridge behind the operator seats which allowed her to observe situations with an unobstructed view. She maneuvered her chair into position, whereupon metallic clamps rose from the floor and grabbed onto the wheels, locking them in place. That portion of the floor then rose three feet into the air, allowing her to see out the entire canopy window.

The man at the left control console in front of her said, "Ma'am, the other White Army aeroships have taken off and are assuming attack formation."

"The fools," she said. "Initiate Slugword Beta." Slugwords were secret codes Bronte-Astrape Enterprises placed into all their technology which allowed them to take control of anything they manufactured. And they had manufactured all the White Army's technology and most of the Tesla Towers in Russia.

"Initiating Slugword Beta," he confirmed.

Ahead, the White Army aeroships taking up formation above Winter Palace suddenly stalled. They veered into one another before dropping onto the Palace like lead weights. The building literally caved to the pressure being put on it, sending columns of smoke into the air, briefly obscuring the view. When it cleared, the smashed vessels lay among the rubble, and from up here they looked like toys a child had thrashed during a tantrum.

With that taken care of, Grimfall turned her attention to the left armrest in her chair. She tapped a button, and a screen popped up. On the screen was a map with a large, pulsating white dot representing Anastasia Romanov. Strange—it was twice as large as normal. She studied it for a moment and eventually noticed it wasn't pulsing regularly—there was a barely perceptible second pulse, indicating the presence of another Awakened. Whoever they were, they were traveling with the young Romanov.

Grimfall grunted in irritation. Someone new had entered the picture, someone with unknown abilities.

"Should we pursue the Romanov girl now?" This question came from her business partner and second-in-command Nikola Tesla, who stood off to her right. Now in his sixties, he was legally blind and carried a cane with built-in Sonar to help him get around. He had been recruited by Grimfall from the very beginning, and together they had revolutionized energy worldwide.

She briefly considered the situation. "No. Another Awakened has joined them. We need to analyze the situation before taking further action. We'll withdraw for now. Once we have a clearer understanding, we can initiate Slugword Alpha."

* * *

Nelly parked the truck in front of a communal apartment building in Petrograd. "What are we doing here?" Ana said.

Nelly explained, "In order to acquire the diesel we needed to come here, I had to make a deal with a fuel station attendant. In exchange for the diesel, I agreed to check on her sister. This'll just take a moment. Grigori—I'm counting on you to protect Ana." Nelly pointed at the former grand duchess and hugged herself.

He replied in Russian.

"He says he will keep me safe."

"Good," Nelly said. "I'll just be a minute." *Hopefully*.

She got out and went through the front gate whereupon she found herself in a maze-like inner courtyard composed of hedges. It took her several minutes to navigate through it to the building proper.

When she finally managed to enter, she emerged into a dark, tight corridor. The ugly brown walls were rotting away, and the place reeked of moldy wood. "Hello? Is there an Alyona Petrov here?" No answer. "Alyona Petrov?"

From a room up the hallway on her left, an old woman hobbled out. She resembled an Egyptian mummy with her wrinkled, leathery skin and emaciated frame. She wore a blue shawl and walked with a wooden cane. She peered at Nelly through obvious cataracts. "Who is there?"

"My name is Nelly Flowers. Zenaida Petrov asked me to come check on her sister. Her name's Alyona."

The woman hobbled over to her. "This is strange place for an American."

"I realize that, and I will leave quickly. I just need to know if Alyona is all right."

"She is not here. The Whites took her a few weeks ago. We do not know her fate."

"Oh." The taste of bitter disappointment turned Nelly's stomach. "I see. I'm sorry to bother you."

The old woman explained, "I am her grandmother. Alyona is... special. The Whites want to exploit her abilities."

Alyona was an Awakened, then. "Do you know where they took her?"

"*Nyet*. It would have been foolish of them to tell us."

"All right," Nelly said. "Zenaida will be crushed to hear that, but I promised to tell her how her sister is doing."

She left the building and they then drove to a communications office and sent the message to Zenaida.

* * *

Kapitan Joseph Stalin sat at his seat in the Bone Smasher X's cockpit surrounded by half a dozen operators and crew members. The space was twenty feet long and ten feet wide. The machine rumbled mightily as they headed toward their destination, the darkness illuminated only by the weak overhead lighting. Stalin, despite being securely buckled, found himself jostled every which way. Yurovsky sat next to him, the latter coming along to correct his failure and help them end Anastasia Romanov. Not that he would be much help, but a man must clean up his own messes.

"Sir!" one of the operators behind him said. "We have intercepted a communication from the Whites. Anastasia Romanov had been picked up by them earlier."

"Drat!" Stalin said. "We are too late, then."

"Actually, no. There was some sort of battle afterward and she escaped in a truck with an attached trailer. They were last seen heading northwest across Palace Square. Curiously, the truck is an American model."

Stalin gave a wolfish grin. "We still have a chance, then. Take us to Petrograd and have our contacts in and out of the city keep us abreast of any sightings of the truck."

"Yes, Kapitan!"

Stalin turned to address Yurovsky. "It looks like your failure may be corrected after all."

Yurovsky said nothing. He simply stared ahead nervously.

The Bone Smasher X shook again as it adjusted course to go after Anastasia Romanov. Stalin decided he would be very happy when he didn't have to ride in these things again.

Glava 8

Nelly, Ana, and Grigori had been conversing for some time, and Nelly felt she had gotten to know him pretty well. Admittedly, some facts about him she could have gone without knowing, but she was eternally grateful for his help.

They now traversed Primorskoye Highway northwest of Petrograd toward Raivola with forest on either side. There had been no sign of pursuers since leaving Palace Square, but Nelly worked her jaw up and down while her fingers drummed incessantly on the steering wheel. She still had much anxiety she couldn't wait to get rid of.

Suddenly, the truck began shaking, and Nelly fought to keep it on the road. The vehicle careened left to right and back to left as she struggled to get it under control.

"An earthquake?" Ana said, her voice higher than normal. "Ours are the worst in the world, I'm told."

Nelly furrowed her brow anxiously. "I don't think so. The shaking appears confined to us; the trees up ahead aren't shaking."

Ana closed her eyes and began murmuring.

Be our protector,
Our faithful companion,
See us off!
Bright and charming,
Life under skies,
Known to our hearts,
Shine in our hearts!

"What's that?" Nelly said.

"A Russian prayer," she replied.

"I don't know what's going on right now, but I'll take any divine intervention we can get."

Grigori, amazingly, had fallen asleep and began snoring loudly. *Just what I need.*

The shaking intensified and Nelly looked around to try and find the source of the disturbance. She glanced in the rear-view mirror in time to catch a terrifying sight. Behind them, the ground exploded upward in a shower of soil and concrete, and some sort of giant machine rose like the fabled Kraken beneath the sea.

Time seemed to slow down, and she got a good look at it before it landed on the road. It was large—perhaps three times the size of the truck and trailer combined. It had a silver color and was some sort of vehicle as it sped forward on huge treads. It took up both lanes of the highway.

Nelly, certain she had seen something like this before, thought back. Anything as crazy as this would only have been seen during her first adventure. Something... something in the prison. What was it? It then hit her: Grimfall's Bone Smashers. Nelly had seen those tunneling machines in Garasheth's underground prison. The monster had been planning on digging a tunnel from Death Valley to California to sneak his army of prisoners in and take over the state, the first step in conquering mankind.

That had been several decades ago. Grimfall had obviously updated her design since then because this machine had *two* giant drills attached to the front instead of one like the early models had.

"What is that?" Ana shrieked.

"One of Grimfall's machines," Nelly replied, trying to sound cool and collected.

"It came out of the ground!"

"It sure did."

Nelly dropped her foot on the accelerator like a multi-ton weight. The truck shot forward, but Nelly had no idea how fast the Bone Smashers could go. They had only gotten a brief glimpse of them in Garasheth's prison.

To her horror, the tunneling machine accelerated as well, and now its twin drills closed in on the trailer. If anything happened to it, the truck wouldn't fare much better since they were joined together.

Nelly's eyes darted all around in search of someplace they could maneuver to dodge their goliath pursuers, but the Bone Smasher took up both lanes and the area on either side was thickly forested. From what she could tell, the trees were too thick to enter the forest.

Was there a way to unhook the trailer without stopping? She didn't think so, and even if there were, the behemoth behind them would probably shred it like paper without slowing down in the slightest.

She considered other options. Maybe they could bail out and run into the woods on foot? She shook her head. The odds of them pulling that off without getting turned into bloody pulp were exceedingly slim.

A sudden blow rocked the truck as something—presumably one of the drills—bore into the back of the trailer. An unholy grinding noise tore at their eardrums while Nelly fought to get ahead of the enemy.

Grigori yelled something, meaning he must have awoken. "He wants to know what's going on," Ana said.

"We're being chased by a crazy machine," Nelly replied, stating the obvious.

Ana relayed the information to him, and he gaped at the passenger-side rear-view mirror. He then yelled something else. "He says he'll deal with it."

"What?"

But he had already opened the door and he clambered onto the side of the trailer.

* * *

He didn't know what this crazy contraption was, but he would not let it harm young Anastasia. Grigori pulled himself up onto the trailer roof and spent a moment orienting himself to being on top of a moving vehicle, swinging his arms about to keep his balance.

The trailer's rear door had been shredded and now hung awkwardly in numerous pieces of twisted metal. The vile monsters obviously weren't satisfied with that because the machine continued pressing forward, digging deeper into the trailer inch by inch. A shower of sparks flew off all sides of the trailer's rear end. No time to waste, then.

Beyond the drills, there was a relatively flat roof on the enemy vehicle. Wasting no more time, he took a running step forward and leaped over the drills and onto it.

All right, I am here. Now what? His eyes scoured the roof for some sort of entryway. At first, he didn't see any. But after a few moments, he noticed a round handle jutting out which had been blending into the roof as it was all the same color. He knelt and tried turning it. Not surprisingly, it was locked. Well, that wouldn't stop him!

Veins popped up all along his arms as he strained to rip the hatch off. He bared his teeth and roared in animal fury. Within moments, the hatch came off with a metallic scream and he hurled it into the forest which shot by in almost a blur.

Something whipped past his cheek, drawing a thin line of blood. Must have been a bullet. It didn't matter; nothing would stop him from stopping *them.*

He reached into the hole and took hold of the first person he could get his hands on by the neck. He proceeded to yank him out of his seat and held him up, the man's lower body still inside the machine.

* * *

Ana leaned out the passenger side window of the truck and gawked at whatever was happening behind them. From her position, Nelly couldn't see it. "What's he doing?" she asked.

"He's on top of the... um... 'vehicle.' He found a hatch and he's trying to rip it off." A few moments passed. "He got it off! Now he's reaching inside. He's pulling someone out! It's—"

She suddenly went silent. Nelly glanced over at her. Ana's face had gone deathly pale. "What is it?" Nelly said.

Ana started shaking. "It's Yurovsky! The man who murdered..." She trailed off, unable to finish the sentence. After a few more moments, she found her voice again. "Uncle Grigori! Rip his head off!" she wailed.

"We need to stay focused," Nelly said. "The priority is stopping that machine before it turns us into human cocktails without the glass."

Ana pointed an accusing finger at her. "That's *your* priority! Mine has just changed. I will see justice for my family."

* * *

These weren't the Whites, Grigori realized. The man whose neck he currently had his hands wrapped around was Yakov Yurovsky, a member of the Reds. This wasn't that Grimfall person, then. It was that bastard Lenin trying to finish the atrocity he began. No matter—they would fail! Despite flailing about wildly, Yurovsky may as well have been a fly for all the strength he possessed.

Grigori's next thought was to pull Yurovsky completely out of the machine and hurl him off it, but someone below must have been holding on to him because Grigori faced stiff resistance. Fine, then.

Grigori let go of one side of Yurovsky's neck and clubbed him over the head with a meaty fist. The cur's eyes rolled back, and he collapsed back into the machine.

He decided to drop down into the vile contraption and deal with however many enemies lay within, but then something slammed into his shoulder and sent him reeling backward. One of those dogs had gotten a lucky shot off.

Grigori fell backward onto the edge of the roof and found gravity a harsh mistress. Despite the incredible pain, he managed to dig his fingers into the metal side through brute force and create handholds. He hung off the side of the machine.

Glancing over, his determination was renewed by the sight of the drills having gotten through a third of the trailer. There wasn't much time!

His bullet wound sent a crashing jolt of pain through his body as he pulled himself back onto the roof. It felt as though his shoulder had been dipped into a volcano, but pain be damned! He would protect Anastasia at all costs.

Once back on the roof, he charged over to the hatch and dove in headfirst. This resulted in him coming facedown onto a still-unconscious Yurovsky. This would, of course, do nothing to remedy his condition. Grigori slid off Yurovsky's lap and onto the floor, finding himself in between chairs. This was the cockpit, then.

Confused shouting erupted along with a series of gunshots. The space was dimly lit, however, and Grigori's black clothing helped him blend in with the shadows.

Grigori pushed himself up off the ground in time to catch an enemy lifting a gun to his head. Grigori delivered a thunderous fist into the man's gut, rocketing him into the wall. Grigori then snatched up his pistol.

Someone grabbed the tsarets from behind and wrapped some sort of wire around his throat. The assailant squeezed and the garrot sliced into Grigori's throat, threatening to decapitate him. *You want my head? You can have it!*

Grigori drove his rock-hard cranium into the man's noggin, causing the enemy to drop like a sack of Russian potatoes.

"That's enough!" a man said in Russian. He looked to be in his late twenties or early thirties and had a light beard. The pips on his uniform indicated he held the rank of Kapitan.

Three more men stood on the other side of the cockpit pointing Fedorov Avtomat automatic rifles at him. He didn't know if he could survive a barrage from all three. He held the gun behind his back.

"To whom am I addressing?" Grigori replied in Russian.

"I am Kapitan Joseph Stalin, leader of Comrade Lenin's Special Operations Unit 23."

"Kapitan Joseph Stalin, you will leave Anastasia alone," Grigori said firmly.

"My mission is the eliminate her, and you are in no position to make demands. I applaud your courage in coming to face us alone, but that is counterbalanced by your utter stupidity." He suddenly cocked his head inquisitively. "I know you. You are the Mad Monk, are you not? You're supposed to be dead."

"My fate is for God to decide."

Stalin laughed. "I'd say now is a good time for him to make up his mind. If we shoot you and you die, he has decided, has he not?"

"I cannot argue with that." He had already located the operator of this infernal machine: the only man still seated at the controls to Stalin's right near the rear of the cockpit. Grigori brought the pistol forward, leveled it at the poor sod's head, and pulled the trigger.

But Grigori Rasputin was no firearms expert, and this turned out to be an automatic pistol. The recoil caused the spread to go wild, putting dozens of holes in the wall and none in the operator himself.

However, this scared the operator enough to dive out of his seat, leaving the driller unattended. The machine lurched violently, and the floor tilted at a most unnatural angle, causing everyone to fall over.

* * *

The Bone Smasher veered to the right, broke free of the trailer, and crashed into the forest, annihilating a copse of trees before coming to a stop pointing upwards at about a seventy-five-degree angle atop the resulting debris. White smoke with wisps of black tendrils billowed up from the two drills which stopped moving within moments.

Nelly hit the brakes and the truck lurched to a stop. She and Ana spent several silent moments staring back at the crashed machine.

"W-We should go make sure Uncle Grigori is okay." Was that what she really wanted, or was she more concerned with finishing off Yurovsky? Honestly, Nelly couldn't blame her if it was the latter.

"I'll get out first. You stay behind me, and we'll approach *carefully*." Ana nodded.

Nelly grabbed the electro-rifle off the dashboard, opened the door, and stepped out onto the highway before coming around to the passenger side. She motioned for Ana to follow, and Ana did so. Together, they crept over to the wreckage of the Bone Smasher, electro-rifle aimed and ready to fire.

They stopped within a few yards of the mechanical abomination which hissed and crackled, while the occasional spark shot from the drills. The treads had been torn loose so this thing wasn't going anywhere anytime soon.

"Privet?" Ana said, her raised voice causing Nelly to jump. "Dyadya Grigoriy? *U tebya vsyo* v poryadke?"   There was no response. Nelly didn't know what to do, as no ladder could be seen on this side of the Bone Smasher. Was there any way to climb up? Was climbing up and peeking in even a good idea?

Nelly jumped again when Grigori popped his head out of the hatch, yelling something triumphantly in Russian. He pulled himself out of the machine, reached back in, and produced the unconscious form of Yurovsky. Grigori hopped to the ground with Yurovsky on his shoulder and unceremoniously dropped the murderous Red onto a tree stump. The jolt woke Yurovsky whose eyes burst open, and he began raving in his native tongue while flailing about to get away. In his battered state, however, he would be going nowhere.

"Yakov Yurovskiy," Ana said in a venom-suffused voice. *"Ty ubil moyu sem'yu,"* she then said accusingly.

"Mne zhal'! *Lenin prikazal mne likvidirovat' tsarskuyu sem'yu. U menya prosto ne bylo vybora!"* Yurovsky yelled in a futile attempt to appease Ana while trying to wave the three of them off.

"My dolzhny ubit' yego," Grigori said to Ana.

She nodded. "Yes, we must." To Nelly, she said, "Give me the rifle."

"What? No. What are you thinking?" Nelly said.

"Uncle Grigori is right. This man needs to die for what he's done to my family."

But Nelly replied, "You're emotional. You're not thinking straight. Killing him won't bring them back."

"Give it to me!" Ana screamed and lunged for the electro-rifle. They grappled for a few moments, although Ana was a skinny teenager; she had no hope of overpowering Nelly. But as Nelly looked into the girl's crazed eyes, she realized she had no right to tell Anastasia Romanov how to act in this situation. After all, no member of Nelly's immediate family had ever been gunned down in cold blood.

"Fine." Nelly let go and Ana took the rifle. She took a few steps back, clearly not wanting to fire it off at close range.

"Ya umolyayu tebya! Szhal'sya! Szhal'sya!" Yurovsky pleaded with her to spare him.

"And how much mercy did we receive from *you?"* Ana said.

"Ya bol'she nikogda i nikogo ne ub'yu! Obeshchayu!"

"I know you won't kill anyone ever again. That's because I'm going to kill you myself."

Yurovsky started bawling. "Nyet! Nyet! Nyet!"

"On the contrary," Ana said. "Da."

Yurovsky managed to get to his feet and tried to hobble away, but Grigori took hold of him by the collar and threw him back to the ground.

Ana's stare bore into Yurovsky, her icy demeanor promising suffering. *Was it truly the right decision to give her the rifle?*

Ana trembled as she tightened her grip on the weapon. She inhaled and exhaled as if she were underwater struggling for a lifesaving breath. Her jaw went up and down and left and right, exposing pristine white teeth. Tears cascaded down her face.

"Are you sure about this?" Nelly said.

Ana didn't answer. Rather, she kept her gaze locked onto Yurovsky, agony etched onto her face. This went on for several minutes.

Finally, Nelly calmly walked over and took hold of the rifle. Ana relinquished it with neither fight nor argument. The former grand duchess simply turned around and walked back to the truck. Grigori furrowed his brow in confusion but followed her without protest.

Nelly looked at Yurovsky with a mixture of pity and disgust. "I don't know if you can understand me. But you're very lucky. I don't know if I would have done the same thing in her position. Count your blessings and consider a new line of work."

He continued to stare at them in wild terror before taking his chance and running off into the woods.

Nelly went around to inspect the damage on the trailer. The rear wall was gone, and jagged pieces bent hideously at dangerous angles on what remained. Thankfully, all four wheels remained intact.

She got back in the cab where Ana and Grigori waited. Nelly drove off hoping never to see another Bone Smasher ever again.

At first, they continued in silence. Finally, Ana said, "Did we do the right thing?"

Nelly replied, "We're still alive, the villains failed to kill you, and Yurovsky faced some measure of justice. I consider that a victory."

"That wasn't what I asked."

"Strategically, we did the right thing. Morally? Only you can decide that."

The silence resumed while they continued toward Raivola.

Interlyudiya

Five years ago.

Victoria Grimfall sat at her workstation in her aeroship's lab soldering wires into her latest electronic device. Bronte-Astrope Enterprises had come so far since its founding in 1891, due in no small part to her recruiting of Tesla, and construction continued on her ultimate headquarters.

Although now in her late forties, she still found herself powered by youthful energy and ambition, always eager to propel mankind into the future in a never-ending quest for progress. True, in her youth, she had done some questionable things, but those days lay behind her now, and the future was brighter than ever.

As she applied the solder to the wires, a spasm broke out in her hand, causing her to hiss as the white-hot substance burned her. Groaning, she went over to the medicine cabinet and applied ointment to her hand.

These spasms and other muscle failures had begun recently. Sometimes her hand slipped while working, and her tripping because her foot acted up increasingly concerned her. She made the decision then to have it checked out.

* * *

She barely registered the words at first. It may as well have been an out-of-body experience for how unbelievable it was. For all her intelligence, she couldn't process the information. "What did you say?"

Her aeroship's onboard doctor explained, "You have amyotrophic lateral sclerosis. It's a progressive neurodegenerative disease which causes nerve cells in the brain and spinal cord to atrophy."

She had heard of it, of course. They taught it in med school, but it was an exceedingly rare disease and she never expected to contract it herself. She remembered very few of its finer points.

She took a deep breath to compose herself. "Very well. What is the treatment?"

She would never forget the look on his face. It crushed her with its complete hopelessness. "I'm sorry, but there's no cure. It will continue to spread until it destroys the muscles in your mouth and lungs making you unable to eat and breathe. You have approximately five years to live."

Victoria Grimfall had always taken pride in remaining cool and detached in bad situations. But the next thing she knew, her fist rocketed several inches deep into the doctor's face. He crumpled to the floor of the med center office, his eyes rolled back into his head.

She trembled and couldn't breathe, so she believed she was dying then and there, and uncontrollable terror gripped her entire being. But she soon realized she was hyperventilating due to extreme stress.

Tesla, who accompanied her, put a reassuring hand on her shoulder, but nothing in this world could comfort her.

Her eyes remained locked on the unconscious form of the doctor as she desperately wished she could trade places with him. What she wouldn't give to be blissfully unaware in that moment.

* * *

Over the next few months, she did little other than stare out the window of her aeroship cabin. She managed to find some comfort in peering at the clouds and imagining she had already died, and her soul now rose above the world's strife, and she didn't suffer anymore. She occasionally gave an acerbic laugh at spiritual ideas encroaching into her logical core.

Eventually, her legs deteriorated to the point she had to be confined to a wheelchair, and her arms had begun weakening as well. Thankfully, Tesla proved a deft hand at managing the day-to-day operations of the corporation in her absence.

One day, Tesla suggested she read a newspaper to take her mind off things, and as she didn't have the energy to argue with him, she complied.

She parked herself in front of her window and held the bundle of pages idly in her lap. She moaned sadly, not wanting to do anything other than stare out her window as usual.

After a few minutes passed, she managed to send a signal to her eyes to look down already and the following headline jumped out at her:

Grand Duchess' Purported Healing Ability Stuns Russia

The article was written by a reporter named Nelly Flowers. Why did that name sound so familiar? Grimfall swept it from her mind; the story itself was what mattered.

In it, Nelly reported the claims of those within the Romanov inner circle that Anastasia

Romanov, the youngest daughter of Russia's tsar, could heal her brother's unspecified illness and had actually saved his life on more than one occasion. Their mother, Alexandra, remained adamant the power belonged instead to a holy man named Grigori Rasputin, but as he had reportedly been assassinated, fingers continued to be pointed at the grand duchess.

Grimfall trembled as she read the article, her hands shaking the page almost to the point she couldn't read it. Somehow, she needed to secure an audience with young Anastasia.

But before she could, the Romanovs were deposed and put under house arrest. Grimfall was again crushed, but before long, her old drive and ambition flared up. More stories of other people with superhuman abilities appeared in newspapers. None of them seemed to share Anastasia's ability to heal, but that didn't mean none did. If Grimfall could build some sort of special ability detector, she might be able to find a more approachable healer. But for that, they would need someone to study.

* * *

"Report," Grimfall said to Tesla. They had convened alone in her cabin. She lost the use of most of her muscles, but she could still talk fine.

"We approached the parents of one of the 'Awakened,'" he said.

"Discretely?"

He nodded. "Yes. I made up a fake name for our organization and offered them money to study their son. They... were less than receptive and told me to leave in rather colorful language."

Frowning, she said, "Well, then it's a good thing we didn't reveal the real name of our operation."

"With all due respect, perhaps it would have been better to present them with an established and reputable name."

"No," she said. "Better to be cautious with what I have in mind."

He furrowed his brows in a quizzical expression. "What exactly *do* you have in mind?"

She steeled herself to say what he didn't want to hear. "We're going to take the child by force. Covertly, of course."

"What? That's kidnapping!"

Of course it was. She had successfully banished her less ethical impulses for years, but with her very life at stake, she couldn't afford to play nice anymore. "The ends justify the means. It's my life against a child's comfort. The choice is obvious. You don't want me to die, do you?"

"Well..." He rubbed a hand through his hair. "No, of course not. But we're not criminals. We perform extensive background checks on everyone we hire. There isn't anyone in our employ who'd be willing to risk their job and freedom in such a brazen act."

She flashed him a twisted smile. "Then, we'll have to look outside our employ. We'll hire 'independent contractors' to do the job. No contracts or any other paperwork. We'll pay them in cash. If anyone of them ever talks, we'll deny everything. Yes. We can do this, Nikola!"

His nervous eyes drilled into her. "The child will be returned unharmed, right?"

"Of course. We'll just get what we need and spirit him back home."

* * *

She rubbed a loving, shaky hand over the six-foot-tall metal box in her lab. Finally, the Awakened Detector was complete.

She flipped the ON switch and the screen in the middle of the box lit up showing a map of the world that could be zoomed in to finetune results. A few dozen dots appeared across the world. Finally, she could track down all the Awakened.

She smiled.

* * *

Her smile had long since evaporated. They hadn't been able to find a single Awakened with the ability to heal, and with the hourglass almost out of sand, that left only one option. She had to secure Anastasia Romanov.

"That will be incredibly difficult," Tesla said in her cabin. "The Red Army has her locked away thousands of miles deep within Russia. It would take an equally powerful army to get to her."

"Perhaps, but we are very fortunate there's already an army seeking to get to her. We could fund the opposing Whites to free her under the condition they grant me an audience with her."

"Do you think they'd be willing to work for an outsider?"

"Money talks, Nikola. Particularly in an economy that's been devastated by war."

"Very well. I believe our best option is to approach Lavr G. Kornilov. He's loyal to the tsar and would be most willing to accept our help."

"Excellent. Let's pay him a visit."

Glava 9

In Raivola, the trio asked about any outsiders frequenting the area. The townspeople marked a spot on a map for them. Afterward, Nelly drove through the forest northwest of town, taking the trail marked on the map. The trail wound throughout the woods, zigzagging left and right, right and left, before they finally came to the clearing. Sure enough, there was an aeroship sitting on the ground.

Nelly stopped the truck and they all got out. "That is an old model," Ana remarked.

"That's a good sign. But we need to check the name. It should be on the other side." They walked around and they spotted the following etched into the side of the aeroship:

~~Philistine~~ Spring Hope

"This is it!" Nelly said.

Grigori said something and chuckled.

"He wants to know if we should knock."

"Yes, let's do that," Nelly said. They went up to the cargo bay doors and Nelly rapped loudly upon them. "Hello? Is anyone home?"

At first, nothing happened. But then, the doors began opening, eventually revealing a middle-aged man with salt-and-pepper hair pointing a conventional rifle at them. "Who are you?"

The trio put their hands in the air. "Easy," Nelly said. "We don't want any trouble."

"You didn't answer my question," the man said.

Nelly replied, "Jay? That's you, isn't it?"

98

"Huh?" His already suspicious eyes narrowed even further. "How do you know that?"

A voice behind him said, "I believe *I* can answer that." From the shadowy interior of the cargo bay stepped another figure, although unlike Jay, this old man hadn't aged a day. He took up position next to Jay.

"Michael Lazarus!" Nelly said, now smiling uncontrollably.

"Again—how do you know that?" Jay said.

Michael said, "Jay, do you not remember the long-lost fourth member of our group? Granted, she is an adult now, but surely you have not forgotten her."

Jay lowered the rifle. "Nelly? Is that you?"

Nelly nodded gleefully. "Yes! It's me. I've wanted to see you guys again for so long!"

Jay and Michael descended the ramp and embraced Nelly. "It's been so long! I didn't think we'd ever see you again," Jay said. His face was weathered now, and his figure had gotten pudgy over the decades, but he still had much light left in his eyes. In addition, he no longer had his crazy beard.

"Indeed," Michael said. "We were not even certain if you ever made it back to your family from Pleroma." His appearance was the same as when she had last seen him. Not surprising, since he was an immortal Gnostagar.

"Yes! I made it back and we participated in the Land Run and that was super scary too! I almost got sucked up by a tornado, but we managed to avoid it!"

"Doesn't that beat all!" Jay said. "You had another adventure we didn't know about."

"Well, you know *now*." Nelly looked past them to the interior of the cargo bay. "Where is Miss Eva?"

All the happiness drained from Jay and Michael's faces instantly. "She's... not here," Jay said.

"Oh," Nelly said. "Will she be back soon?"

"We do not know," Michael said. "We can talk more inside."

"Oh—who are your friends?" Jay said, evidently only now noticing Ana and Grigori.

"Jay, Michael, may I present Anastasia Romanov, the grand duchess of Russia, and her, um, good friend, Grigori Rasputin."

Jay's eyes bugged out. "The princess?"

"As my father was not a king, I am not a princess, although the difference is minor. Nice to meet you both."

"We have never met royalty before. It is a pleasure to make your acquaintance. And to you as well, Grigori Rasputin," Michael said.

"Privet!"

"Uncle Grigori says hello."

"Come," Michael said. "Let us go inside. We have so much to catch up on."

They all went inside, and Jay closed the cargo bay doors. Nelly remembered when they had all been imprisoned in here. Now, the place had been turned into a recreation room with a parlor table game (from English inventor David Foster) in the center of the room. This had interchangeable parts, allowing people to play cricket, football, and lawn tennis. Also, a punching bag hung from the ceiling.

"You've really improved the place since Garasheth ran things," Nelly said.

"We had to replace the cockpit canopy after jettisoning it to kick him out. It was crazy! Eva pulled off the most insane maneuver I've ever seen, and to this day she still hasn't topped it," Jay said.

"You'll have to tell me all about that," Nelly said. She then turned to Michael and said, "I'm sorry things didn't work out between our two peoples."

He shrugged. "The governments of the world wanted information we could not give them. We Gnostagar decided as a species we would let humanity guide its own path. Couple that with the natural enmity of nations like Austria, and it proved too insurmountable an obstacle to overcome. My people returned to Pleroma, and I alone remained."

"I don't mean to be rude, but we need to move quickly," Ana said.

"Yes, yes, sorry," Nelly said. To Jay, "Do you guys remember what that tree told us when we passed the Trials?"

Jay rubbed the back of his head. "Uh, something about the full potential of the human brain getting unlocked."

"Yes! And now it's begun. These two here have been Awakened. They have powers. And get this—that mad scientist Dr. Grimfall is after them!"

"That lady with the crazy white face and electrocuted hair?"

"That's right. But now she's dying, and she wants to dissect Ana's brain so she can heal herself."

"Well, we cannot let that happen," Michael said. "We must stop her."

Nelly nodded. "Exactly! We need to get out of Russia, and we need your help to do that. I wouldn't ask if it wasn't a matter of life and death."

Jay began stroking his chin. "That's going to be tough. We're stuck here because all Russian airspace is guarded by Tesla Towers. If we try to fly out, we'll be shot down immediately. We need all hands on deck here."

"Yes," Nelly said. "We need Miss Eva. Where is she?"

Michael sighed. "I am afraid we had a falling out."

"What do you mean?" Ana said. During this conversation, she had been quietly translating for Grigori.

"Nelly, do you remember when we were in the Akasha Archives and Eva found that book which disturbed her so?" Michael said.

"Yeah, kind of."

He explained, "That book revealed the future. There was to be another great war a few more decades from now. That war would be started by a man named Adolph Hitler and would ravage the world—her native Austria included. Miss Eva could not accept this, and so, without telling us, she spent years plotting his death before he could seize power. Not long ago, she carried out her act. Jay and I were outraged, and we admonished her severely. Consequently, she left the ship."

"Oh, my god," Nelly said. "Where did she go?"

"She's been hanging out at a bar in town," Jay said.

"I'll go talk to her. Can you guys look after my new friends here?"

"Certainly," Michael said, as cordial as ever.

"Thank you. And listen. If any black aeroships show up, you'll have to defend them."

"We don't have that much in the way of weaponry. There's Eva's cache, but she doesn't want us using them," Jay said.

"You might not have a choice," Nelly said. "But hopefully, I'll be able to bring her back quickly."

* * *

Nelly drove back into town and found the bar Jay was talking about: a ramshackle affair with a door falling off its hinges. Not exactly indicative of royalty, but then again, neither was Eva.

Nelly pushed the rusty door aside and entered. The interior was dark and reeked of cigarettes. Nelly waved the smoke out of her face and examined the room.

It didn't take long to spot the only woman in the room. She was much older now, but that was definitely Eva Lamarr. She still wore her dark brown duster coat and cowboy hat, only now they were dirtier than Nelly remembered, and her hair had thin gray streaks in it.

Nelly sat down beside her at the bar. "You look like you've seen better days."

Eva put down her glass but didn't glance over at the newcomer. "We've *all* seen better days. What's it to you?"

Nelly shrugged. "Just looking after a friend."

Eva turned her head to examine Nelly. "Who the hell are you?"

Laughing, Nelly replied, "You dropped me out of an aeroship and can't even remember my name? You defended me from rapists at Death Valley and you don't know me?"

Much like Jay, Eva's jaw dropped. "N-Nelly? Is that you, kid?"

"Well, I'm not a kid anymore, but yes. It's great to see you again, Eva."

Nelly had never known Eva to be particularly affectionate, but now the Austrian royal exploded from her seat and hugged the latter fiercely.

"Oph! That's tight," Nelly said. The other people in the bar began to gawk at them.

"Sorry, kid. It's just that you arrived at a hell of a time. I could use a friend right now."

"You *have* friends. You've had the same friends since 1889. And you'll *always* have those friends."

Eva shook her head and returned to her chair. "I thought Jay and Michael were my friends, but they turned against me after I eliminated the greatest monster the world will ever know and saved the day again."

"Yes, they told me. But you obviously knew they wouldn't approve, or else why wouldn't you tell them you were going to do it?"

Eva took another shot and slammed it down on the counter. "Those two have always been uncomfortable with death. Michael because he caused so much of it, and Jay because he's such a softie. But I stand by what I did. Millions have been saved. Do you know what that man Hitler was going to do to people, especially Jews? I'm a goddamn hero."

Nelly said somberly, "Of course you are, Miss Eva. You saved *my* life multiple times in only a few days. You risked yours to stop Garasheth's invasion. You saved the entire world. I don't know whether what you did to this Hitler guy was right or wrong, but you'll always be my hero."

Eva was silent for a moment. Then, "Thanks, kid. I needed that. But what the hell are you doing in Russia?"

Nelly explained everything to her. "And so, you see, I need everyone's help to get Ana and me out of the country."

"Why on earth would I help the tsar's kid? In case you weren't paying attention, they tried to crush Austria in the great war. She can rot for all I care."

"Listen!" Nelly said. "She had nothing to do with that. She's just a kid, and she just watched her family being gunned down in front of her, *and* she almost joined them. Please—she's all alone right now. All she has is us."

Eva poured another shot from the bottle in front of her. "Forget it. I won't lift a finger to help a Romanov. I will only help *you,* Nelly. Buuuut if anyone else happens to benefit from that, I won't complain."

Nelly put her hand on Eva's. "Thank you, Miss Eva."

"Heh. You're still calling me that. You must be at least 40 by now."

"It's not polite to mention a lady's age. Especially since you're older than me."

Eva said, "I've lived my life. I have a lot of regrets but also a lot of things I'm happy I did. In the end, I can only hope the good things outweigh the bad."

"You're a good person, Miss Eva. Jay and Michael haven't forgotten that. Come back to the ship and do one more good thing."

Eva stood up and downed one last shot. "All right. I'll settle my tab and meet you at the *Spring Hope.*"

"Much better than 'Philistine.'"

"Of course! We couldn't let the stench of Garasheth remain."

Nelly laughed at the crossed-out name on the side of the ship and returned to it.

* * *

A short time later, Eva walked up the *Spring Hope's* ramp with clear apprehension. Jay and Michael stood at the top staring at her, and Nelly stood behind them.

They spent a minute staring at each other, no one willing to make the first move. Finally, Nelly pushed Jay and Michael forward and said, "Talk. Now."

The two men rushed over and hugged Eva. "We missed you so much!" Jay said.

"Indeed. We are not whole without you," Michael added.

"Thanks, guys," Eva said. "Just know that I did what I did for the greater good. Millions will be saved because of it."

Jay said, "But then, why didn't you prevent the first great war? You knew how it would begin, didn't you?"

Frowning, Eva explained, "The book didn't impart knowledge so much as show me images. I was only able to work out that Archduke Ferdinand would be assassinated sometime this decade because of the technology I saw around him when he was killed. I didn't know exactly when and I didn't recognize the site where he was killed. But I *did* see Adolph Hitler in a hospital I recognized in 1916 because I'm very familiar with Germany and Austria. It was simply a matter of waiting for him to arrive. Monitoring communications between European nations allowed me to act when that happened."

"So, that's why you spent so much time on comms," Jay said.

"Not entirely," she said. To Nelly, "We spent the war flying over battlefields, dropping supplies, and airlifting troops to safety. The advanced radio system on board this ship allowed us to know when and where we were needed. That much is true. That I happened to also be listening for news of Hitler's admission to the hospital in Beelitz did not interfere with my other duties."

Michael added, "She eventually asked if we could visit the hospital to see if they needed any help. When she returned, she acted as if nothing had happened. Only later when we came to Russia to seek new adventures did she admit the truth. And before we knew it, the country entered lockdown."

"We've been stuck here ever since," Eva said. "But before we go any further, I want to meet Anastasia Romanov."

"We were giving her a tour of the bridge," Jay said.

The foursome went to the bridge where they found Ana sitting at the controls. "Ana, I want you to meet my good friend Eva Lamarr, a member of Austrian royalty."

Ana got out of her seat and bowed to Eva. "Thank you so much for helping me!"

"Let's get one thing straight," Eva said. "I'm not helping *you*. I'm helping Nelly. Your being helped is merely a side effect. The help Nelly gets will trickle down to you."

"I'm sorry. Did I do something to offend you?"

Eva pointed a finger and said, "You're the spawn of Nikolas Romanov who tried to crush my precious Austria in the war."

"But I had nothing to do with that! I hated the war as much as anyone. People blamed my parents for Russia's problems, but they were good people. I won't have you slandering them!"

Eva's nostrils flared and Nelly was afraid she would deck the kid. But surprisingly, Eva said, "You've got fire. They haven't taken *that* from you. Maybe you'll amount to something after all."

Grigori, who Nelly hadn't noticed standing in the corner, came over and grabbed Eva's butt. *"Ochen' myagko!"*

Eva spun around and launched her fist into his face. He fell to the floor in a heap. "Who's this *arschloch?*"

"That's Uncle Grigori," Nelly said, visibly embarrassed. "I was going to warn you about him, but then you insulted my father, and he acted rather quickly, so..."

Eva examined the peasant. "What a disgusting creature! And that smell! Tell me you're not helping this *thing.*"

Nelly shrugged and said, "We're kind of indebted to him."

Groaning, Eva said, "What did he say while he was violating me?"

Ana replied, "He said, 'Very soft.'"

Eva groaned again. "Well, at least I got a compliment out of it. But you make sure to tell him not to do that again."

"I'm pretty sure he understood your message," Ana said.

"Is he always like this?"

"Yes," Ana said. "He used to watch my sisters and me undress before bed."

"What?" Eva spat on him. "You will behave yourself on board this ship! Do you understand?"

"Mne zhal'!" He covered his face to defend against any further blows.

"He says he's sorry."

"Yes, I suppose this cretin has *much* to be sorry for."

Nelly interjected, "Can we return to the topic at hand, please? How are we going to get Ana out of Russia?"

"Depends on where she wants to go," Eva said.

"I need to get to London to reunite with my remaining family."

"London, eh? Hmmm." She went over to a cabinet along the wall and removed a map which she then placed over the operator's console. They all gathered around it. "The Gulf of Finland is about eight and a half kilos from here," she said, pointing to the body of water to the southwest. "We get to that, and we can take it to the Baltic Sea and head west to neutral Sweden."

"Unfortunately, going by sea means we would have to abandon the *Spring Hope*," Michael said.

"Can't you use your connections as an Austrian royal to facilitate safe passage?" Nelly said.

Eva waved her off, saying, "Nah, I cut ties with them a long time ago. Don't get me wrong; I love my homeland more than anything, but I couldn't accept the way my family does business. After all, they made me into a monster willing to casually take lives.

"But I digress. We wouldn't have to abandon the ship permanently. We could come back for it. But Nelly might have to leave her truck here."

"I'm fine with that as long as we can all get out of Russia safely."

"I'm sure I can replace anything that's lost after we get to London," Ana said.

But Eva said, "Sure, as long as what's lost isn't people. We have to do this right. There's no room for error.

"Anyway, our best bet is to head to Koivisto here." She pointed to a port city to the northwest of Raivola. "It's currently controlled by the White Army, not the Red Army, and not Grimfall who are both

109

looking for Anastasia. The city's in lockdown but I doubt they're too keen on helping that white-faced bitch after she backstabbed Kornilov. We go there, and we can charter a boat—legal or otherwise—to take us out of here."

"The sooner we leave here, the better," Jay said.

"Indeed," Michael added. "It behooves us to waste as little time as possible. From what Nelly has told us, Victoria Grimfall is desperate to get her hands on Anastasia as fast as humanly possible."

"Yes. I don't think she has much time," Nelly said.

"I wish I could help her, but I'm not willing to die just yet," Ana said.

"Especially not for that psycho," Eva said.

But Ana said, "I don't think she's crazy. She's facing her own death just as I had to do. I think, if I were in her position, I'd do anything to survive."

Eva pointed a finger at her. "You *are* in her position because she's trying to kill you to ensure *her* survival. It's you or her, and you've chosen correctly."

"But isn't there anything we can do for her?" Ana said.

Nelly replied, "She told us herself. She has the most advanced technology on the planet, and she's powerless to change her fate without taking your life."

"This isn't even worth debating," Eva said. "Our priority is to get to Koivisto which is about fifty kilos from here. I say we leave in the morning."

"Yes, let's do that," Ana said.

"It is agreed, then?" Michael said.

"Fine with me," Jay said.

Grigori asked something in Russian.

"You shut up!" Eva said.

"Looks like it's settled, then," Nelly said. "We'll all get into my truck and head off."

Glava 10

The next morning, they all gathered outside the truck. "What the hell happened here?" Eva said while gawking at the damage to the trailer.

Sighing, Nelly said, "Yesterday was a long day. I'll explain on the way. Everyone, just... try not to fall out."

They piled into the truck and trailer and set off. Nelly and Eva rode in the former, while the others sat in the latter. They headed southwest on the Roschinskoye Shosse highway toward Raivola on 41K-90, a two-lane road lined by forest on either side.

As Nelly drove, the two women talked. "What happened after we parted ways last time?" Nelly said.

Eva explained, "The tree transported Jay and me back in time to when we were on the *Philistine* being transported to that damned prison, only this time, we weren't chained up. We stormed the bridge and dealt with Garasheth in explosive fashion. Funny thing is, you weren't there, and that bastard didn't even remember you. Not entirely, anyway. He seemed to only have a vague idea that something was off."

"Interesting," Nelly said. "The tree transported *me* back to my parents, only *they* didn't remember me being kidnapped. The timeline definitely changed, but only those of us who met the tree remember what originally happened. Everyone else only has inklings of things being different."

Eva nodded. "Yep. We're in an exclusive club. We should call it the Rememberers Club."

Laughing, Nelly replied, "Nobody remembers better than us! But now that I think about it, Michael remembers, and he didn't meet the tree."

"Who says he didn't? Yeah, he wasn't with us when *we* met the tree, but he seems to have met him later. He doesn't like to talk about his failure to forge a long-lasting bond with humans."

"Did the tree know all this was going to happen?" Nelly said.

"Who knows? The leafy fellow implied the future was yet to be written."

"We should name him!" Nelly suddenly decided.

"Oh! Oh! How about 'Green Godface'?"

"He didn't really have a face…"

"Doesn't matter! I want him to be Green Godface."

Nelly laughed so hard she couldn't breathe. The truck began drifting between lanes before she could get herself under control. "All right! All right! He's Green Godface…" She sucked in a deep breath. From the woman who brought us 'Cherry Bishop.' I knew that name was fake the first time you said it."

"You did not! I picked that name after much thought and consideration. It was foolproof."

"Until you told us it was fake, you mean."

"Fair enough," Eva said. "So, what happened to you, kid? What's your life been like?"

Nelly said, "After the Land Run, my family settled down in a brand-new town called Guthrie, Oklahoma with hundreds of other people. Before long, they built a schoolhouse, and I got back to studying. I stayed in Guthrie until I turned eighteen, at which point I ventured off to Central State Norman School, the state's first university.

I wanted to stay informed of everything that happened in the world because of our adventure, so I majored in journalism. After I graduated, I worked for various newspapers until finally landing a job at the New York Chronicle. My latest assignment brought me to Russia, and here we are."

"Did you start a family?" Eva asked.

"Yes! I got married and we have a son. We named him Michael Evan Jay Rosenbaum after you guys."

Eva stared at her for a moment. "My name's not Evan."

"Well... yeah, but 'Eva' isn't really a name for a boy."

"Unbelievable! Have you forgotten what the Trials had to teach us? Boy; girl; doesn't matter. Just be who you are."

Nelly shot back with, "True, but there are these little bastards called bullies and they love nothing more than boys with girl's names."

Eva chuckled. "Don't lecture me about bullies. I've met the finest this world has to offer. But... I'll concede the point."

"Ha, ha, thank you. So, what has *your* life been like? As far as I can tell, you never married."

"Nah. For whatever reason, I'm not attracted to anyone. I don't feel sexual desire. Not sure why. Oh, and there's the fact I don't want kids. Not that I despise the little buggers; I just don't want to bring up a child in this broken world."

But Nelly said, "I don't think the world's without hope. After all, Green Godface told us of the potential the future could hold."

"Yeah, well, he also told us nothing is set in stone. Paradise isn't guaranteed by any means. We have to make it ourselves, and a hell of a fine job we've done so far. No, I'm not dragging any youngsters into this hell. Hitler may be gone, but we never know when the next monster will appear—

especially since I made such a massive change to the timeline."

"Well..." It was hard to argue with that logic, but Nelly wanted to say *something* encouraging. But, why? Eva had made her choice, and it was a perfectly reasonable one. Just let it be. Besides, she wasn't attracted to anyone, anyway. "Okay. You make a good argument."

"I wonder if things turned out differently in the other world," Eva muttered.

"What?"

"Nothing," she said. "Just thinking to myself."

What was she talking about? What other world? Did she mean Pleroma? "As far as I know, all the other Gnostagar went home except for Michael."

Eva laughed. "Tells you what terrible sense he has. Could have gone back to a nice, infinitely large, cozy house where no one ever dies."

"Although, there is the occasional torture pod," Nelly said, grinning.

"Is there? We never actually saw any," Eva said. "I wonder if they just made that up to scare us."

Nelly replied, "I have to believe if Garasheth and Shabalesh could have created such a thing, they definitely did."

"Touchè."

* * *

Tesla entered Grimfall's cabin aboard the *Potential*. The room itself was basically a second laboratory for her. Besides her specially-designed bed, her cabin consisted of a lab table with a high-powered microscope, beakers full of various fluids, and a back-lit radiographic display above. There were also other diagnostic machines as well as devices that boosted Grimfall's mobility such as a mechanical skeletal frame.

Currently, the doctor lay on her bed, her wheelchair off to the side. "Yes, Nikola?"

He cleared his throat and clasped his hands behind his back. "Anastasia and her friends are headed northwest. We believe they are going to Koivisto to attempt to escape by sea. If that happens, they'll be out of range of our towers."

"That would be unfortunate," she replied. "Is Subject Zeta ready?"

"For the most part," he said. "There are a few... quirks in the programming, but it should work fine as long as we don't overtax Zeta."

"Excellent. In that case, initiate Slugword Alpha immediately."

There was silence for a moment. "Understood."

Grimfall scrutinized him. "Is something wrong, Nikola?"

"It's just..." he started. "Are we truly doing the right thing? Murdering a child?"

"It's for the greater good," she said. "We can save millions of lives if we can improve upon Anastasia's power. What is one life against the entirety of the human race?"

He chewed his lip nervously. "Are you doing this for mankind... or for yourself?"

"I will not be lectured here. I created all of this. I made you what you are. I could have chosen Edison for my revolutionary enterprise, but I saw your greater potential. Do not threaten the faith I have placed in you, my dear Nikola."

"Very well," he said. "I apologize, Victoria." He bowed and left.

He was a good man, but this situation called for ruthless men. It ate at her, but evil needed to be done to save her.

* * *

Later that afternoon, the group arrived at Koivisto. It was a heavily wooded town interspersed with buildings. The real sight was the dock on the city's southeast side. It consisted of a dozen piers with boats and ships of all different sizes.

Nelly drove the truck through one of the winding roads that led through Koivisto and soon arrived at the marina. She parked and they all got out.

"Okay, Anastasia Romanov," Eva said, "you and your lecherous friend are the only ones here who speak Russian and I don't trust that perverted ragman, so you'll have to do the talking for us."

"You can count on me."

They began canvassing the piers to find a suitable ship to leave on. They tried booking themselves as passengers but found no one wanted to risk violating the lockdown.

Eventually, though, they found an old-style steamer and managed to convince the captain to hire them on as crew members until they got to Sweden. They shook hands with him to seal the deal.

And then the ground started rumbling.

"What's that?" Nelly said.

"An earthquake?"

Looking around, Eva said, "I don't think so. You hear that hum? And Jay, the hairs on your arm are standing up."

"You are correct," Michael said. "And look at Grigori's beard!"

The Russian lecher's mass of facial hair was pointing upward and obscuring his face. *"Chto proiskhodit?"*

The hum abruptly stopped, and everyone's hair went back to normal.

"That was very strange," Ana said. "What in the world—?"

She was cut off by a series of booms happening all around them followed by a high shriek and then...

"Oh, my god!" Nelly yelled.

Hundreds of feet in the sky above, a red web of pulsating energy sprang up and covered the city, blocking off their access to the sea.

And then a high shriek battered their ears, and a voice began speaking out of nowhere.

Anastasia Romanov! I know you can hear me. I am transmitting through the vibrations in the air. All of White Army-controlled Russia is now cut off from the rest of the world. I know you went to Koivisto to try and escape, but it's useless. Come to me and fulfill your destiny as mankind's savior. I'll even allow you to travel by aeroship but know that it will be sliced to ribbons if you try to breach the web.
I'll be waiting for you in Moscow. You have 24 hours.

The high-pitched whine stopped, though Nelly's ears now rang like a gong.

"Jesus Christ!" Eva said. "Can't that bitch communicate like a normal person?"

"I don't think she's *ever* been normal," Jay said, contorting his head as if he could relieve the pain that way. The people around them were muttering excitedly and looking at the energy web with fear.

"Indeed," Michael said. "But the important thing now is young Anas—"

He stopped and they all stared at Ana. She stood pale as a corpse, staring at nothing with wild eyes.

"Ana?" Nelly said, suddenly scared for the former grand duchess.

"I can't escape," Ana said. "I'm going to die. That woman is going to kill me. I tried to be brave, but having hope and then watching it get cruelly taken from me..." She broke down in wailing sobs.

Nelly hugged her tight. "It's okay! No one's dying here. We'll go to Grimfall, and we'll put an end to this."

"If there's an ass that needs beating, I'll beat it," Eva added.

"We're with you all the way!" Jay said.

"Of course," Michael said. "Despite everything that has happened, I cannot abandon a human in need."

"*YA ochen' smushchen,*" Grigori said.

Ana managed a weak smile. "He says he's very confused." She then relayed to him what was happening.

"*Bog ispytyvayet nas. My budem nastoychivymi,*" Grigori said with a look of firm conviction.

"He believes God is testing us, but we will persevere."

Nelly nodded vigorously. "Someone who is not my ancestor once said, 'The power of the human spirit is in living when all you want is death.' We're going to show Victoria Grimfall the power of the human spirit."

"We'd better get moving, then," Eva said. "We don't know how long Clownface is going to wait around."

Nelly laughed. "You are so good at naming people."

They left the very confused captain and returned to the truck. By this point, most of the citizens had retreated into their homes. For all they knew, the deadly crisscrossing pattern above them was liable to rain down lightning.

Glava 11

They got back to the *Spring Hope* after night had fallen and reconvened in the cargo hold. They stood in a circle to strategize.

"Okay, Grimfall wants us to come to her, but she didn't tell us her exact location, only that she's in Moscow," Jay said.

"She wants us to find her, so she won't be hiding," Eva said.

"She has given us a day, so we should prepare, I think," Ana said.

Michael said, "That is a good idea. But we do not know anything about the good doctor's lair or what defenses she might have."

Nelly explained, "She has enough black aeroships to make Farahilde Johanna proud." She winked at Eva. "Her mercenaries use electro-rifles. When we met her in Garasheth's prison, she also had giant tunneling machines."

"Those antiques are nothing," Eva said. "She now has the ability to seal off thousands of kilometers of a sovereign country and track Anastasia wherever she goes."

"Well, what do *we* have?" Ana asked.

In response, Eva whipped out her pistols and twirled them. "We've got my old Colt Lightnings. We've got a few other guns and plenty of ammunition, but we're *vastly* outnumbered."

"We still have a half dozen sticks of dynamite," Michael said.

"True," Jay said. "But without knowing anything about Grimfall's hideout, we have no idea how to use them."

Nelly noticed the gears turning in Eva's head. "Or do we?"

Eva said, "There is one possibility—the old coralite missile launcher."

"That would level all of Moscow!" Michael said.

"We don't even know if that bomb still works," Jay added.

Perplexed, Nelly said, "Are you talking about that thing Garasheth used to blow up Washington? He already used it, and he said that was the last of it."

"Ah, ah, ah!" Eva said, wagging her index finger. "He *used* to have used it. But we changed history and stopped him, which meant we got the warhead. In fact, it's right behind you."

Nelly turned around and for the first time noticed a steel crate the size of three suitcases put together. "You're telling me it's in there?"

Grinning wolfishly, Eva said, "Open it up and see for yourself."

Nelly reached out but her hand wavered. "I don't want to disturb it."

"Setting aside the fact we still have it, and even if it still works, we would kill hundreds of thousands of innocent people if we set it off," Michael said.

The wagging continued. "Not if we took most of the corallite out of it and left just a tiny piece. We could contain the blast to a small area."

"If the corallite is even still functional," Jay said. "And the middle of a battle is a bad place to test that."

Wag! "Farahilde studied coralite extensively upon returning to Austria from Washington. She discovered it has a half-life of fifty million years. And it's been on this planet only since 1431. In other words, it'll still be explosive long after we're gone."

"That's... good. I think..." Nelly said. "But does the launcher still work? I'm guessing you haven't used it."

Eva put her hands on her hips and puffed out her chest. "Oh, ho ho! We *have* used it."

Jay nodded. "During the war, we figured out a way to launch relief packages with it. It was very clunky since the packages weren't the exact shape the launcher was designed for, but we made it work."

Eva began counting on her fingers. "We have the coralite, it still functions, and the launcher still works. I'd say we're ready to do this."

"Let me see if I understand this," Ana said. "You have a weapon you can use against Grimfall, but it is very dangerous."

"Only if we don't scale it right," Eva said.

"Which could very easily happen," Michael reminded her. "We have no idea how much coralite to remove, especially since we do not know the size or location of Grimfall's base of operations."

Nelly thought about it for a moment. "Could we find that out and then scale the bomb?"

Eva said, "Sure, although it's not the most comfortable experience. You see that hatch over there?" She pointed to the middle of the floor. "You open that up, and you can drop down and meddle with the launcher. Just make sure you put on the safety harness first. Otherwise, you'll fall to your death."

Nelly's stomach lurched. "Oh, god. You mean... one of us has to go outside during flight?"

"Is that a problem?"

"Well..." How could she put this delicately? "Ever since you dro—got me out of that aeroship as a kid, I've had a terrible fear of heights."

Eva grimaced. "I'm sorry. Believe me, if there had been any other way, we would have taken it."

"It wasn't your fault. I would have died up there if not for you."

"Thanks," Eva said. "And don't worry; I never meant for *you* to go down the hatch."

"I won't lie, that's quite a relief."

Eva walked past her and opened up the crate. An all-consuming green light emerged and lit up the cargo hold. "She's a beauty!" Eva grinned from ear to ear. "We'll go in, take out Grimfall, and get the hell out."

"Do we really have to kill her?" Jay said.

"I'll admit, it doesn't sit well with me, either," Ana said. "I never thought I'd become a killer."

Eva replied, "It's you or her. From what you've told us, she's too desperate to just let this go. She won't stop until she has your brain in a jar."

Jay and Ana looked around nervously but could offer no alternatives.

"Very well, then," Michael said. "We should all try to get some sleep. Tomorrow promises to be eventful. I share our friends' distaste for bloodshed, but Miss Eva is correct. Victoria Grimfall is dying, and she will do anything it takes to change that."

Ana relayed to Grigori all that had been said.

"Budet mnogo shuma?" he said.

She nodded. *"Ochen' mnogo shuma!"* She put her hands together and then spread them apart while mimicking the sound of an explosion. Grigori's normally penetrating eyes were wild with excitement.

Eva said to Ana, "I need you to do your best to impose upon him the seriousness of tomorrow's mission."

Ana's right hand shot to her forehead in a salute. "You can count on me!"

Eva looked at Grigori with disgust. "It's *him* I'm worried about."

Ana and Grigori began going back and forth on the plan. He seemed to be taking it seriously. His eyes were locked on Ana, and he kept nodding vigorously.

"I think he'll be all right," Nelly said after scooching over to Eva. "If it weren't for him, we never would have escaped from Grimfall. He's got a hell of a story to tell to boot. It's got attempted murder, a drowning, multiple chases, court intrigue, *another* attempted murder... well, you get the idea."

Eva rolled her eyes. "If he gropes anyone else, all the stories in the world won't save him. I've seen how he looks at members of the fairer sex aboard this ship. He is a *perversling,* and I don't think you need me to translate that."

"Give him a chance," Nelly said.

"If I wasn't giving him a chance, he would already be dead," Eva pointed out.

Nelly laughed. "Fair enough. So, what moniker have you, The Queen of Names, come up with for him? I know you've got something better than 'perversling.'"

"Even *I'm* not vulgar enough to say that out loud."

* * *

The next morning, Nelly left her cabin and entered the bridge to find everyone waiting for her. "I take it no one else could sleep, either?" They all nodded.

"Are we ready to take off?" Eva said. Again, they all nodded. "Well, then, here we go."

Everyone got strapped in. Eva and Jay manned the controls while Michael was seated at the communications console. Nelly, Ana, and Grigori took their seats near the bridge entrance.

125

Eva pushed a few buttons before pulling back the throttle. A low rumbling began which increased over a minute. "You okay, kid?" Eva said to Nelly.

"I'll be fine!" Nelly replied perhaps a tad too loudly. She had intended to display cool confidence just like her faux ancestor Jeanne de Fleur. In actuality, she felt more like her *real* ancestor Gabrielle Deschanel, the conflicted former assassin. Was she doing the right thing here? Would any of them even survive this? As a kid, she'd had no choice but to go along with whatever reckless plans other people had, but now that she was an adult, the responsibility for the lives of her friends was a crushing weight.

If Eva noticed her doubts and unease, she didn't say anything. "Okay, then! Here we go."

The *Spring Hope* lurched off the ground and gradually gained speed as it rose to the heavens. When they had reached a comfortable height—above anything on the ground but well below the energy web—Eva put them on a southeast heading toward Moscow which was almost 700 kilometers away.

All the while, Nelly was jostled every which way in her seat by the turbulent ride. Regardless of who won today, the real loser might end up being her stomach.

* * *

From her command ship *Potential*, Grimfall pressed a button on her wheelchair, and one of the screens in front of her activated revealing an unconscious figure lying on a bed in Medbay 3: Subject Zeta.

This was one of her insurance policies to insure the retrieval of Anastasia. Her scientists and engineers had worked tirelessly to enhance Zeta's strength while eliminating free will. In short, Zeta functioned as an automaton, a weapon to be directed at whatever Grimfall pointed to. Hopefully, Zeta wouldn't be needed, but the soldier's presence reassured the doctor.

She activated the comm unit on her wheelchair. "Grimfall to Medbay 3."

On the screen, one of the doctors in scrubs pressed a button on the wall next to a speaker. "Yes, Director."

"Our guests are about to arrive. Activate Subject Zeta in standby mode."

"Understood." He walked over to where Zeta lay on the bed and began motioning. Grimfall couldn't see his mouth moving because of the surgical mask, but she remained confident her orders would be carried out.

Glava 12

They arrived on the outskirts of Moscow around noon. None of them were in any mood for lunch. Even if they had been, what they saw hovering above the Kremlin would have surely extinguished it.

"What the hell is that?" Nelly shouted.

"It is an aeroship," Michael said.

"That's way too big to be an aeroship!" Jay said.

Indeed, what loomed on the horizon before them more closely resembled a floating city. It *looked* like an aeroship, certainly—being cylindrical and metallic—but it must have been ten miles long and three miles wide. Countless gun emplacements covered the exterior. A massive ring of thrusters encircled the front of the aeroship. The word *Potential* was emblazoned on the hull in hundred-foot-tall characters.

"If we take that thing out, a lot of people below will be killed," Eva said.

"So, what are we going to do?" Ana said.

Eva explained, "Our only chance is to blow a hole in it and go inside to face Grimfall directly."

Suddenly, the dreaded communique sounded again:

I am running out of patience. Come around to the stern immediately for docking.

"I will never get used to that!" Jay said upon taking his hands off his ears.

"You won't have to," Eva said. "We're ending this. Michael, take the controls and bring us to her stern. I'm going to ready the missile."

"Aye-aye, Miss Eva," he said before sliding in to relieve her.

Eva said, "Anastasia, you and the perversling are with me. I'm going to need his strength to quickly get the bomb into the missile."

"Right!" She relayed this to Grigori and they both got to their feet. The three of them then ran into the cargo hold.

* * *

Eva had Anastasia act as her translator while she instructed Grigori. "First, reach in and remove the bomb from the crate."

He grunted in exertion as he did so before setting it on the floor.

"It normally takes three of us to lift that thing, so your incredible strength comes in handy today."

She opened the casing to show the bomb itself was composed of hundreds of shards of coralite organized into groups of twenty bundles. She removed bundles until only a few shards remained. "There. That should be enough to damage Grimfall's flying fortress without downing it."

Eva instructed Grigori to carry the bomb over to the hatch on the floor. A system of intersecting ropes hung from the ceiling. "Next, we'll get you in the harness. Don't try anything funny while I'm working on you."

Grigori put one leg through the harness followed by the other. Eva brought more ropes under his armpits and secured them.

Once it was done, Eva opened the hatch. The screaming wind shot in from the outside and whipped their hair about. "Okay, now sit on the edge of the hole with your feet dangling over it." She had to shout to be heard over the cacophony. "Now, grab the bomb and ease yourself down the hole.

"This next part is very important. All you have to do is insert the bomb into the missile that's mounted on the underside. Don't worry about removing the head of it; I've already done that. Just push the bomb into the missile's interior."

With a mighty shove, he did as instructed. Eva then lowered a cylindrical metallic cone, and he took it. "Finally, just screw that onto the missile's body."

When it was all done, Eva pushed a button on the wall initiating the hydraulic system that lifted Grigori back into the room. They got him out of the harness and Eva closed the hatch.

"I certainly wasn't expecting to say this, but good job, Grigori."

He nodded proudly, his hands on his hips.

* * *

Michael maneuvered the *Spring Hope* over to the stern of Victoria Grimfall's gargantuan vessel. Nelly watched as docking clamps unfolded from the *Potential* and moved toward them. Nelly couldn't help but feel like a sailor facing the tentacles of the fabled Kraken.

Eva, Ana, and Grigori returned to the bridge. "Don't let those docking clamps get us," Eva said.

Michael backed out of range of them.

"Are we ready?" Nelly said.

"To show that bitch what we think of her? Absolutely!" Eva said. "Michael, take us out to 500 meters and point the prow at those docking clamps. We're going to fire the missile right there."

"I'm not a tactician by any means," Ana said, "but shouldn't we target the bridge? That's where Grimfall is most likely to be."

Eva shook her head. "Taking out the bridge would most likely bring down the whole thing and kill lots of your people below. Not to mention, the engines are near the bridge, and they would almost certainly be destroyed. We need to throw them off balance while keeping them afloat."

The deck shifted beneath them as the *Spring Hope* veered away from the *Potential*.

WHAT ARE YOU DOING??

"Shutting you up, for one thing," Jay said, groaning.

Michael brought the ship around and pointed the prow at the rear of the *Potential*. "Miss Eva, are you certain you have properly adjusted the amount of coralite needed to do this without killing us?"

"Nope."

Nelly sighed. "Wonderful."

"Everybody, take your seats and buckle up!" Eva said. Once they had all done so, she said, "Fire!"

Jay worked a series of buttons and levers at his station. Another klaxon sounded on the bridge, and the whole aeroship began rumbling. The *Spring Hope* was then rocked by the firing of the warhead. Nelly bit her tongue which resulted in sharp pain and the taste of blood.

Eva, Michael, and Jay had witnessed the full destructive power of the coralite bomb decades ago as they had a front-row view at the time, whereas Nelly had only seen a green glow from the window of the cabin Garasheth had locked her in.

A glowing green ball rocketed forth from the underside of the ship, a smoke trail in its wake. It struck the stern of the *Potential* and emitted a blinding green light that enveloped the bridge's canopy windows. There was an unspeakable roar of an explosion and rending metal, and the *Potential* lurched slightly. Flaming debris fell from the enemy ship as molten slag.

A moment later, the *Spring Hope* abruptly spun out of control as the shockwave hit them. "Stabilize!" Eva said from the communications station.

"I am trying!" Michael said.

Nelly's stomach lurched when the view in front of her was entirely replaced by the ground below—or in this case, directly in front of them.

Somehow, in the middle of all this, Eva managed to get to Michael's station through a combination of crawling and flying and got the ship to stop spinning. But they were still plummeting to the ground. "Jay! Increase thrust!" she shouted over the unholy ruckus.

Jay did so, and she leveled the ship, bringing it back up right before it smashed through one of the Kremlin's towers which they missed by mere inches.

Nelly, dazed, saw a pile of orange-green liquid at her feet and realized she had puked during the turbulence. She wiped the remains from her lips with her sleeve.

Eva brought the *Spring Hope* back around and to a stop in the air. "Is everyone all right?"

"Yes, I think so," Ana said.

"'All right' might be subjective, but I am unharmed," Michael said.

"I'll be fine, I think," Jay said, his head wobbling.

"Hey, we got reinforcements," Nelly said woozily. "There are three of each of you."

"*Vokrug menya vsyo kruzhitsa!*" Grigori stared at the ceiling, probably to avoid looking at any duplicates or whirling scenery.

"Okay, sounds like no serious injuries," Eva said.

Nelly's vision stabilized and they stared ahead at the *Potential*. A gaping hole a hundred feet tall and probably twice that wide had been ripped in the massive aeroship's stern. Jagged pieces of hull jutted up and down from it like the teeth of a monster.

"How do you like that!" Eva shouted, although Nelly didn't know if Grimfall could hear them. "That's how Eva Lamarr gives a bloody nose."

"Now what?" Nelly said.

Eva replied, "Now, we go in there and shut her down. It'll be me and Grigori since I need Michael and Jay to stay here and keep the ship afloat. The perversling can at least back me up."

But Ana said, "I'm going, too."

"The hell you are!" Eva said. "You want to just go ahead and hand yourself over while you're there?"

The former grand duchess stood resolute. "I won't stand by while others are fighting for my sake. I want to confront Grimfall personally and make her stop myself. I will keep my life in my own hands until the end, and that means not cowering on this aeroship."

Eva sighed. "Fine. But from a strategic viewpoint, this is a very bad idea. You don't normally take the victim to the murderer."

"If she's going, I'm going," Nelly said. "I feel responsible for her. I've still got the electro-rifle I took from one of Grimfall's henchmen and it's got a full charge. I can cover you."

Eva began massaging her temple. "Do you have any experience with guns, kid?"

Nelly puffed out her chest. "I grew up in Oklahoma! We hunted regularly to stay alive."

"An electro-rifle's a lot different than a hunting rifle," Eva said. "The lightning can arc in unpredictable ways."

But Nelly replied, "I know that. I once did a story on Bronte-Astrape Enterprises and the research required me to learn how to use many of their devices, the electro-rifle included."

Anastasia Romanov! It will take much more than that to stop me. You will come to me even if I have to pluck your antiquated aeroship out of the sky and drag you in here myself!

"Okay, okay!" Eva said. "We'd better go while we still have eardrums left. Michael, Jay, as soon as we board her ship, get out of here. We'll signal you when we're ready for you to return."

"Signal us how?"

"Errrrrr…" She frowned as she mulled it over. "We'll communicate the same way Grimfall's been communicating."

"Please, don't," Jay said.

"Fine, fine," Eva said. "We'll figure something out. There has to be normal communications equipment over there somewhere."

"Let's go before the desperate doctor does something drastic," Nelly said. Ana nodded.

Eva nodded right back. "All right. You three, come with me to the cargo hold."

They went to the rear of the ship where Eva opened a series of panels in the ceiling revealing four lengths of rope. "We're going to have to rappel down into the hole we just made in Grimfall's ship. Everyone, take a rope and get ready to jump," Eva said.

A thought suddenly occurred to Nelly. "There isn't radioactive fallout or anything from the blast, is there?"

"Nah, coralite is clean energy. It was never even considered as a possible weapon until Garasheth came along."

"Okay, good. That's a relief," Nelly replied.

The *Spring Hope* shifted beneath them, and they all hung onto the ropes to keep their balance. Within a minute, the ship stabilized again.

Eva went over to a panel next to the door to the hallway and pressed a button. "Michael, are we in position?"

His tinny voice came through the speaker. *"Affirmative, Miss Eva. But the* Potential *has launched smaller attack craft and they are converging on our position. You must hurry."*

"Roger."

Next to the panel was a lever and she pulled it down. A klaxon sounded—because of course it did—and the rear doors creaked open. A rush of wind embraced them and now they all had a good look at the damage they had just caused.

Through the open hole, a half-collapsed deck loomed. Fortunately, most of the fires had now gone out.

Eva pointed to what remained of the deck, indicating they were to rappel onto it. She went first and slipped down there like a pro. Ana and Grigori went next while sharing a rope—he put one meaty arm around her and grabbed the rope with the other before leaping like a madman from the cargo hold. Somehow, he managed to avoid slipping, though the rope burn must have been horrendous. They touched down on the deck next to Eva.

Her nausea crept back as she realized it was now her turn. Taking a deep breath, she took hold of the rope and emitted a scream to psyche herself up. It worked—sort of. She ran to the floor's edge but panicked at the last moment. She ended up falling off and initiated a death grip on the rope.

Now dangling from the ship, she spied aeroships half the size of the *Spring Hope* coming in from the other side of the *Potential*. Climbing back up wasn't an option, so she scrambled down the rope, her adrenaline flowing like the Cimarron River. Nelly let out incoherent cries while shimmying down the rope.

"Nelly! Nelly! It's okay! You made it," Eva said.

Looking down, Nelly was surprised to find herself on the ruined deck of the *Potential*. The rope was abruptly ripped out of her hands when the *Spring Hope* took off to avoid the pursuit of the smaller craft.

The four of them now stood together in front of a door. Behind them, the deck dropped off into a void, beyond which the ground below was visible. "Come on! We need to get going!" Eva said.

They opened the door and proceeded into the *Potential*.

Interlyudiya 2

May 1895 (Infini Calendar), Guthrie, Oklahoma

Nelly returned home from school and dropped her backpack onto the floor of her bedroom before collapsing onto her bed. It had been another rough day in the brutal world of high school, and while she remained steadfast in her belief young adult women in the future would have a much easier time, it couldn't help her at the moment.

She put on a grim smile as she thought about what she would tell her future grandchildren someday. *When I was your age, I had to walk three miles to school because our town was still new and away from civilization. We had homework every night, not like you with your automatic learning devices. And we had to pick our significant others carefully because no one had yet invented a machine to pair people.*

She, for one, couldn't wait for the boyfriend-picking machine, because John was being a pain as usual. Her parents wanted to meet him, but he kept putting it off because he feared offending her father. Nelly also feared him offending her father by refusing to meet him because that would naturally make things difficult between them. And, of course, Snotty Susan wanted John for herself and had been doing her best to get him to secede from the Nelly Union.

Yes.

High school was the worst. Somehow, shape-shifting monsters bent on world domination had been far easier to deal with. She would take a life-threatening ride in a failing aeroship over a teenage clique any day.

She stretched, got up, and turned on the radio on the table under the window. They lived in a wooded area in front of Cottonwood Creek. Through the trees could be seen the newly built Santa Fe Depot, Guthrie's only train station. She found the two-story red brick building comforting because it connected the town to civilization.

A man's tinny voice emanated from the elliptical wooden box. *"Continuing today, we present the next phase of the Senate Hearing on Potential Human/Gnostagar Diplomatic Relations. We now go live to the Senate floor as Senator Art Meadows is questioning the Gnostagar representative Michael Lazarus."*

The broadcast then cut to Meadows' voice. *"You claim to come bearing the proverbial olive branch, but all we have seen are mere pleasantries. What do you actually have to offer us?"*

Michael's soothing, sophisticated voice oozed out of the radio. *"I can certainly understand humanity's skepticism. After all, we have caused unquantifiable damage to them over the centuries."*

"'Unquantifiable damage' is an apt description," Meadows said. *"Your original incursion into our world began in 1431, and by your own admittance, you infiltrated world governments and manipulated the course of human history through abominable actions that include deception and murder. I have prepared a list of known instances of Gnostagar interfering with our affairs.*

"July 1789, France. A Gnostagar called the Count of St. Germaine replaces the Duke of Rochefoucauld-Liancourt and attempts to murder the royal family. Although he was stopped before he

could carry out this unconscionable act, he had already taken a number of lives. How many, we may never know, but it is a historical fact that he disposed of the crew of the royal family's aeroship."

Michael sighed. *"Regrettably, that was the work of Momagesh, one of the members of our original expedition. He infected Maximilien Robespierre with his blood which allowed the French leader to utilize abilities similar to our own."*

"Indeed," Meadows said. *"Some of our people looked into weaponizing your bodily fluids, but the transformations proved to be extremely unstable. No doubt Robespierre's body wouldn't have held up for much longer, anyway. Still, that doesn't change the fact he went on a killing spree in order to obtain large quantities of blood which he added his own altered essence to."*

Although she couldn't see it, she pictured Michael nodding. *"Yes. And I admit I was fully compliant with Momagesh's scheme. We all were."*

Meadows cleared his throat. *"Let's move on. A few years later in 1792, one of your people launched a much more brazen attack, this time here in our capital. He transformed a large portion of Washington D.C. into a mirror of your world Pleroma. Again, he was defeated.*

"July 8, 1853. Your people struck again, this time in Japan. A Gnostagar tried to replace the shogun and gain total control of the country. He, too, was defeated.*

"April 15, 1889. A Gnostagar going by the name Robert Stone, who had infiltrated our anti-Gnostagar agency Heretic, initiates what would be the final attempt to invade our world. We thank the Good Lord he was stopped like the others."

"Yes," Michael said. *"I saw to it personally that he did not succeed."*

"Perhaps," Meadows said. "But let's talk about your actions in these machinations. By your own admission, you murdered the real Abraham Lincoln and intentionally started a war between the Union and the Confederacy. How can you possibly defend this?"

Now, she imagined Michael shrugging sadly. "I cannot. My actions were beyond reprehensible, and I must live with them for all eternity. I will not ask your forgiveness. I am merely asking for peaceful relations between our peoples after centuries of bloodshed and manipulation."

Meadows sighed. "Mr. Lazarus, I'll be frank. The only reason you're here and not in prison or a government laboratory is because of your assistance in stopping Robert Stone and his allies. You cannot expect us to simply forget and forgive. Many of your victims are still alive and here with us today." A chorus of boos and jeers erupted. "I will remind everyone to be civil. This is being broadcast via radio to the entire country, so please refrain from cursing.

"Now, then, Mr. Lazarus. Why should we trust anything you say? Furthermore, how can we be sure no members of the President's cabinet have been replaced by your operatives?"

Michael replied, "I can assure you, I am the last surviving member of the original expedition."

"That may be, but you were able to open the door to our world more than once. Who's to say less like-minded Gnostagar haven't snuck in while you weren't looking?"

"A fair question. The door is guarded round-the-clock—so to speak since time does not exist in Pleroma—and only my chosen representatives are allowed to enter."

Meadows pressed further. *"But what if your trust is not entirely well placed? Even among close human friends, betrayal is rarely out of the question. After all, you betrayed Robert Stone when you sided with humanity."*

Michael explained, *"I have lived with my people for untold eons. I know each one of their hearts. I have taken precautions to make sure no one who is not completely on our side can approach the door. And I do not consider my actions a betrayal. Under the circumstances, they were tragically long overdue."*

"Indeed, they were. Thank you, Mr. Lazarus. No more questions."

* * *

The next day, Nelly tuned in again for the next round of questioning. This time, it was Senator Marianne Bradley's turn.

She began, *"Mr. Lazarus, you said you knew to steer America into the civil war of 1861 because you possess the ability to see the future. Is this correct?"*

"Yes, it certainly is. As I have stated, Pleroma exists outside of time, and as a result, we are able to view any point in history. We even have an infinitely large library called the Akasha Archives. It contains all the knowledge in the universe."

"Interesting," Bradley said. *"And you can access this knowledge freely?"*

"I must stop you right there, Senator. I know where you are going with this line of questioning, and I am afraid I cannot help you with that."

"*Mr. Lazarus, please understand. With complete knowledge of the future, we could prevent all future wars and global tragedies.*"

"*Senator, before we decided to pursue diplomatic relations with humanity, we all agreed to never do anything to warp your path ever again. If we told you everything that is to come and you successfully avoided hardship, mankind would grow weak and complacent. I do not mean to be harsh, but things are coming you must be strong to face.*"

Bradley countered, "*We wouldn't need to be strong if you would just tell us what to prepare for.*"

"*That is simply not true, Senator. For one thing, there are billions of years left in this universe, and we cannot look up every conceivable threat. We Gnostagar have only concerned ourselves with Earth; we do not know what may lurk among the stars.*"

"*But surely you can give us a forecast for the next century or so.*"

Nelly pictured Michael shaking his head. "*We cannot. Our desire is to correct the damage we have done to your path, not influence it further. The decision is not even mine to make, but that of a higher authority.*"

"*A higher authority? Do you mean God?*"

"*I am forbidden from assigning labels to our leader, and in any case, I do not know enough about him to even attempt it.*"

Bradley said, "*You are far more advanced than humans. A being fit to rule over you must be a god by our standards.*"

"*Perhaps. I will not fault you for looking at it that way.*"

"If you do not have the rank necessary to authorize access to the Akasha Archives, would you ask your leader on our behalf?"

But Michael explained, *"Our leader has forbidden any further interference in human history. He would undoubtedly refuse such a gross perversion of the natural sequence of events."*

* * *

The next day, the hearings concluded with Senator Paul Rankin. *"Mr. Lazarus, I still fail to understand what exactly you are offering us. You refuse to share knowledge of the future with us; thus, I am at a loss as to what we can gain from this proposed relationship."*

Michael replied, *"We Gnostagar are the very building blocks of the human psyche. We have much to teach you about your own psychology and mental makeup. Understanding one another will make you a more compassionate species."*

Rankin laughed. It was a cantankerous noise with a Southern drawl that more resembled a crow's cawing. *"Compassion, Mr. Lazarus? The United States has no need for that. What we need is military and technological might to fight off all aggressors, and Bronte-Astrope Enterprises has already made several astonishing leaps in that area. I see absolutely no value in being friends with the Gnostagar. You claim to be mere parts of us, so I would say that makes us your masters. You should obey us without question."*

Ridiculous! These people had no idea who Michael Lazarus truly was, nor did they understand the sacrifices he had made for mankind. Michael was more human than anyone. No senators had been present when Nelly and her friends saved the world, so they had no right to judge.

Not a day went by where she didn't think of her ragtag band of misfits. She would have given anything to see them again. At that moment, she made a decision. She would take a job that would allow her to follow their exploits, and if she could ever make the stars align, they would one day be reunited.

In the end, the result of the hearings was what she expected. The United States rejected the Gnostagar's olive branch, and the rest of the world followed suit. The visitors returned to Pleroma, Michael Lazarus presumably going with them.

But Nelly knew better. Michael would never abandon humanity, even if they rejected him. He would keep fighting for everyone, and the best place he could do that was with Eva and Jay. Nelly became a reporter and kept tabs on her friends as they continued to make headlines with their daring deeds. Being a journalist gave her access to sources and information most people didn't have and taking a job at a major New York publication expanded her resources even further.

Then, one day, the editor-in-chief went around the office looking for volunteers to go to Russia.

Nelly smiled.

Part 2

Bryukho zverya
[Belly of the Beast]

Glava 13

"What is going on?" the booming voice of Victoria Grimfall shouted over the PA system in the Command Center. She meant to be even louder and angrier, but her ailment kept her voice suppressed.

The *Potential* didn't have a bridge; instead, it had a cavernous room for the vital functions of the crew to be carried out. A football field long and three stories tall with multiple balconies, the Command Center stood as a monument to the doctor's accomplishments. No one else in the history of mankind had built anything close to the *Potential*. The ship itself could be perpetually powered by thunderstorms without ever needing to land. There was only one place in the world the juggernaut *could* land—a specially-built dock twenty miles off the coast of San Francisco.

Grimfall sat on her raised platform above the bottom level, Nikola standing beside her. Like most of the crew in the Command Center, she had a computer console in front of her. Unlike everyone else, however, she had a microphone sticking out into which she could issue orders.

The Command Center didn't have a canopy window. Rather, it had a series of glass screens that curved downward from the ceiling and displayed feeds from the various cameras mounted all over the hull. Presently, the feed displayed the hole made by whatever explosive device Anastasia Romanov's outdated aeroship had deployed against them.

"Good god!" Nikola said. "That was a coralite explosion. I've never heard of such a thing. I thought all the coralite had been used up decades ago."

Grimfall studied Anastasia's aeroship and certain suspicions crept in. She couldn't be certain because billowing black smoke obscured much of it. "Zoom in on their ship."

One of the operators on the many stations on the floor below pressed a button. The screen enlarged on the antiquated aeroship, and the word *Philistine* was briefly visible—though crossed out—on the hull in between breaks in the smoke. "I knew it," she said. "That's Director Stone's old aeroship. He had a coralite bomb built to wipe out Washington, D.C., but that ship disappeared in April 1889. I'd be fascinated if I wasn't enraged."

The ex-*Philistine* took off to the east and the Vulture attack crafts gave chase. "Make sure they know to be careful and not kill Anastasia Romanov before the Director is ready for her," Nikola said.

"Roger!" someone shouted.

Grimfall gritted her teeth which resulted in a painful crack. "We're running out of time, Nikola. I don't want to die."

"Nor do any of us want you to."

"I remember when I was fresh out of university. I had such a bright future ahead of me. I thought I had all the time in the world. But our best days slip away from us, and eventually, every one of us must face our end. Some people accept their fate, but I have chosen to fight and claw. I will not go to my grave without exhausting all possible solutions. The world needs my brilliance."

He replied, "You brought the world into the 21st century a hundred years ahead of schedule. You started as a geneticist but then went back to school and got a degree in engineering, a subject you excelled equally at. We are all indebted to you. That is why we serve you faithfully."

"I know if I have just a few more decades, I can take us another century into the future. Isn't that worth the price of a few lives?" Her voice carried a more pleading tone than she intended.

He sighed. "I don't believe I'm qualified to make that call."

"In my youth, I was willing to sell mankind into slavery in the pursuit of scientific knowledge. Now, here I am trying to kill a child just to save myself. I didn't want to go down this path again, but I'm scared."

She pressed a button and spoke into the mic again. "Has the damage assessment on Deck 37 been completed?"

"Affirmative," came the voice of one of her junior engineers, Davis. "I'm right outside the door of Corridor 102 which took the brunt of the explosion. We've successfully sealed it off and re-routed power and fuel to other sections."

"Good," Grimfall said. She decided to put to rest another of her suspicions. "You haven't seen any evidence of intruders, have you?"

"No, Director. And even if someone tried to get in from the other side of the door, we've sealed it tight. No one's getting in here."

"That's a relief. But just to be safe, I want that door double-secured with steel foam."

"Understood! Davis out."

She quickly checked her Awakened detector and found it now showed hundreds of dots everywhere. The dispersed coralite must have been interfering with the readings, something she didn't account for since she believed the green power source to have been long gone.

No matter. She could fix it quickly and find Anastasia.

* * *

Eva took her revolver away from Davis' head. "You did good, boy. Now, get into that room."

Davis and his crew of meek engineers were shepherded into a laundry room by Eva, Nelly, Ana, and Grigori. Eva had her revolvers while Nelly had strapped her electro-rifle to her back before jumping out of the *Spring Hope*. Eva scoured the room for anything that might allow the cowed nerds to communicate with the bridge. There were rows and rows of washing machines and dryers, as well as a first aid kit on the wall, but she seemed satisfied their prisoners would stay put for a while. "Anyone moves, they come out of here with fewer body parts," she said.

Before they left the laundry room, Eva asked Davis, "Are there any hidden nerd tunnels on this monstrosity of an aeroship?"

"N-Nerd tunnels?"

"You know, secret passages where you keep all the wires and guts away from bumbling idiots who might trip on them. Secret passages we could perhaps use to avoid detection?"

"I think you mean the access corridors. Those are tight spaces we go into in order to service the ship's systems."

Eva smiled. "And where might four intrepid intruders find these 'access corridors'?"

The foursome went back into the hallway, a white, stainless-steel affair that was surely spotless before they fired off their coralite bomb. Now, it was caked in dirt and grime and the smell of burning ozone permeated the air.

The door Ana and her friends had come in through had not been sealed. It couldn't even fully shut as it had been warped by the blast. The foursome surprised the engineers when they burst through and held them at gunpoint.

"What now?" Nelly said.

Eva replied, "Simple. We find Grimfall and take her out. She's most likely on the bridge. We'll go in and impose our will on her." Grigori sent his fist into his other hand's palm and said something defiantly. "I don't know what you said, but I like your enthusiasm. Let us handle things, though. If we can get Grimfall to shut off the energy web, we might get out of here without any bloodshed. Big if, but you never know."

"How are you doing?" Nelly said to Ana.

"My heart is pounding furiously, but I'll manage."

"You're doing great, kid," Eva said. "For a Romanov." Ana smiled weakly at this.

They followed Davis' instructions and soon came to a nondescript wall with a rectangular indentation approximately four feet high and three feet wide. Eva pushed it in and slid it aside. The three women crouched and went inside—with Eva in front—while Grigori took up the rear. His larger girth caused him to grunt and curse in Russian while he adjusted to the confined space.

They were now in a dimly lit passageway. The only illumination came from faint green lights—and a few red ones—which ran the length of the ceiling. Nelly guessed they were status indicators; green meant something was working, while red meant it wasn't. To their left, along the wall, were closed compartments that presumably could be opened to service the "guts" inside.

They crawled through the ship's innards for what seemed like an hour, though the unfavorable conditions probably made it feel longer than it was. They remained silent for most of the journey.

Eventually, Ana said, "My knees hurt."

Eva responded, "Bear with it, kid. We can't stop to—"

Without warning, the wall to Eva's right collapsed inward like tissue paper and a pair of hands reached in and grabbed her by the neck before dragging her out.

"Eva!" Nelly said. She scrambled after her friend, but she had been in the glorified tube so long her legs protested the sudden burst of movement. Nevertheless, she gritted her teeth, fought through the pain, and made it to the new hole in the wall Eva had disappeared through.

"What's going on?" Ana said.

"I don't know!" Nelly replied.

When she got to the hole, she found it had ragged edges; someone had ripped it open with their bare hands rather than opening a partition like they had done to enter the tunnel. Upon scrambling out, she was greeted by a surreal scene.

Countless plants of all shapes and sizes filled the very humid room. Some sprouted from pots on tables, while others seemed to be growing from the floor.

Eva stood up against the opposite wall—or rather, was held up by a petite figure with bizarre, stone-like hands clutched around her throat. This otherwise ordinary-looking woman wore the uniform of the *Potential's* crew and was, in fact, shorter than Eva, but somehow had the advantage against her.

Nelly got to her feet and tried to rush over to help the Austrian but stumbled due to the poor condition of her legs. By the time she made it over, Eva was turning blue.

"Let her go!" Nelly said. She wrapped her arms around the young assailant's neck, albeit awkwardly. It was only then that the stranger released Eva—and effortlessly pried Nelly's arms loose in a crushing grip. The attacker then punched Nelly in the chest, hurling her backward to the ground. With all the wind knocked out of her, terror set in as she realized she couldn't breathe. She flailed about trying to suck in air, *any* air.

"Nelly!" Ana appeared and put her hands on Nelly's chest. The pain quickly subsided, and she could breathe again.

"T-Thank you," Nelly wheezed.

Strangely, the woman with the stone hands ceased her assault upon seeing Ana. "Anastasia Romanov." Her voice was stilted and devoid of all emotion. Looking at her, Nelly realized this was no woman. She was a teenager probably even younger than Ana. She looked so familiar... Nelly struggled to remember where she had seen her before.

The woman continued speaking in her robotic voice. "You are my target. You will come with me to the captain."

It suddenly hit Nelly: She looked just like Zenaida. Nelly said, "Are you Alyona Petrov?"

Confusion painted Alyona's face. "I... what is this name 'Alyona'? I am Subject Zeta, proprietary Bronte-Astrape operative."

"No!" Nelly said. "You're Alyona Petrov. Your big sister is worried sick about you. Your whole family misses you and wants you to come home."

Alyona suddenly emitted a cross between a groan and a mournful wail while clutching her head. Her lips drew back, revealing all her teeth. After a few moments of this, a spasm seemed to shoot through her and she stood stiffly, her face having reverted to the icy mask from a minute earlier. "Cognitive conflict resolved. Resuming mission."

She advanced on Ana and grabbed her by her collar. Eva was only just now beginning to recover, so Nelly didn't expect her to make the save this time. However, an inhuman roar sounded behind Nelly and Grigori charged forward, barreling into Alyona and freeing Ana from her clutches. The two went crashing over a table that contained Venus fly traps. When they landed, Grigori groaned as a handful of the carnivorous plants bit into him. Alyona also had a few clinging to her arm, but she didn't look bothered in the slightest. She ripped her sleeves off, revealing it wasn't just her hands that were stone; her entire arms were as well.

Alyona leaped to her feet like an Olympic gymnast and rained stone blows upon Grigori who had not gotten back up yet. He cried out in pain and raised his arms to block the attacks.

Nelly's ears then received a thunderous blow when a shot rang out. Alyona staggered and looked at her arm where a piece had been chipped off. Eva stood there leaning against the wall and pointing her revolvers at the brainwashed Russian teenager. "That's enough!"

Alyona instantly regained her composure and stared at Eva. "Evaluating threat." She looked the Austrian up and down several times. "Threat... negligible."

"The hell did you just say?" Eva said.

"Uh-oh," Nelly said.

Alyona initiated a series of flips and cartwheels, catching Eva off guard and proving her earlier agility was no fluke. When she closed the distance between them, she took hold of Eva's hands and crushed them in hers. Eva cried out and dropped the revolvers before Alyona backhanded her in the face. Eva collapsed and became deathly still.

Alyona turned around and was again confronted by Grigori who hurled wild punches at her. But this time she was ready for him and effortlessly dodged each one. She parried his attacks with movements almost too fast for Nelly to follow. Within moments, Grigori was on his back and Alyona resumed her devastating blows. Blood now poured from numerous gashes on his face.

He fumbled around blindly for something to use as a weapon, and his hands landed on Nelly's electro-rifle. She must have dropped it when she came out of the tunnel. He took hold of it and shoved the barrel in Alyona's face. Alyona raised her arms to block the attack.

"No!" Nelly screamed. "You can't fire it at that distance!"

Either he didn't hear her, or he didn't care. He pulled the trigger, releasing a blistering arc of electricity that engulfed both himself and Alyona, the latter flying backward across the room, skidding across the floor before colliding with the wall. The blistering energy leaped about wildly for a few more moments, shattering a 10-foot-high glass container and sending shards of glass shooting outward like shrapnel.

Silence descended upon the room.

Glava 14

Nelly and Ana rushed over to Grigori who now smoldered on the floor. Smoke rose from every inch of his body, and he convulsed violently. Ana put her hands on him, and he became calm. The electro-rifle sat next to him half-melted.

"Dyadya Grigoriy!" Ana said while visibly fighting back sobs. "Mne zhal'. *Ty pozhertvoval soboy radi menya.*"

"*Ne bespokoysya ob etom. Ya rad, chto smog uberech' tebya,*" he said weakly.

"Will his advanced constitution save him?" Nelly said.

"I don't think so," Ana replied. "The electro-rifle was on the highest setting, and he fired it much too close. I think his healing ability has been over-taxed."

"*Vse khorosho. Ya otpravlyayus' k svoim druzyam. Do svidaniya,*" Grigori said. His eyes closed and he said no more.

The sobs could no longer be held back. Ana wept for her fallen protector. "Why? Why is life so cruel?"

"People make it cruel," Nelly said. "But people can also take away the cruelty. We just have to make the right choices. I'm sorry."

For several long moments, Ana said nothing. Then, "We should probably check on his killer. Make sure she's dead."

"She's not." They turned their heads in the direction of the voice. Eva knelt over Alyona with two fingers on the teenager's neck. At some point, Eva had recovered enough to get up, though her face was swollen with a baseball-sized bruise. Alyona lay prone on the floor. "Her stone arms took the brunt of the attack. Stone is a great insulator."

Ana picked up one of Eva's revolvers, strode over, and leveled it at Alyona's head. She cocked it and prepared to fire.

"Don't!" Nelly said. She rushed over to talk some sense into her friend.

"She murdered Uncle Grigori!" Ana yelled, hysterical now.

"She's not responsible," Eva said. "Clownface brainwashed her. I've seen it before. Brat does hit like a train, though." She massaged her tender flesh.

"She's innocent!" Nelly said.

Ana stood there holding the gun, her arm trembling violently. There was very little chance she would hit Alyona if she fired, but she might hit Eva. Finally, she dropped the revolver and fell to her knees, her bloodstained hands covering her face as she wailed.

Wait... why was there blood all over her hands? Nelly quickly spotted the answer: there was a baseball card-sized shard of glass protruding from Ana's midsection. "Ana! Your stomach!"

Nelly tried getting to Ana as fast as humanly possible, but despite her beating, Eva made it to the Romanov in half the time. "Jesus," she said. "It's pretty bad." Ana continued crying and didn't seem to hear them.

"What do we do?" Nelly said while crouched next to Eva.

Eva gave her a grim frown. "I'm no doctor. Best I can do is rip it out, and I have no idea if that's the right thing to do."

"W-We should bandage the wound," Nelly said.

Eva nodded. "Right." To Ana, she said, "Kid, I'm real sorry about what I have to do here." She grasped the shard with two fingers, but it took several tries to remove it because her hand kept slipping on the blood. Finally, she managed to rip it out. Nelly expected an agonized scream or at least a yelp from Ana, but the teenager seemed to be completely lost in her *emotional* torment.

Eva picked up a dry shard of glass from the floor and used it to tear up her iconic duster into strips. She tied those around Ana's stomach. Only then did the kid stop crying.

"What are you doing?" she asked.

"You've been wounded," Nelly said. "Eva fixed you up as best she could."

"Oh. Thank you." Her voice was distant and sounded almost as robotic as Alyona's.

Sounds of shouting came from outside the door.

"We need to get going," Eva said.

"We can't leave Uncle Grigori here!" Ana said.

Nelly said, "I'm sorry, Ana, but we can't take him with us. We have to get back into the tunnel." She had to prod the former grand duchess to return to the claustrophobic maw, but Ana soon acquiesced. Now it was Nelly at the front, followed by Ana, with Eva taking up the rear to fend off any enemies who came in after them.

Strangely, none did.

* * *

Sometime later, the trio opted to exit the tunnel because their knees couldn't take anymore. They opened a hatch and crawled out into a large cafeteria like the kind one would find at any army base. Florescent lighting beamed down from a low ceiling,

157

and dozens of tables and chairs were spread out across the space. On the far wall were service lines where the crew could get food, as well as condiment stands. No one seemed to be around now, though there were words written on the wall: Cafeteria 12-B.

Nelly got to her feet which wobbled under her weight, but she managed to get stabilized. An equally unsteady Eva popped up next to her. Ana labored to her feet, her chest rising and falling with labored breaths. She had turned pale, and the strips of Eva's duster were soaked crimson.

"Ana, you don't look so good," Nelly said.

"I'll be all right," Ana said, smiling weakly.

"That's right, kid," Eva said. "We just need to get you to a doctor." But the look she gave Nelly conveyed no confidence.

Suddenly, the voice of Grimfall came in through the PA system. "Attention, intruders. You did well to make it this far, even managing to defeat Subject Zeta. I don't want to risk any more of my crew to your violent impulses, so I've ordered them to stay away from you. If you want to find me, come to the Communicarium. It's on the very highest floor. And just so you won't have any trouble finding it, I've sealed off every bulkhead except the ones that lead to it. Come to me and we will end this."

"Ana needs medical treatment!" Nelly said. There was no response.

"Doesn't look like she can hear us," Eva said.

"Should we trust her?" Ana said.

"If she has sealed off all the bulkheads, we don't have much choice," Eva said. "We could keep crawling through the nerd tunnel, but even if we managed to bypass the sealed sections, we don't know the layout of this flying fortress. And all that crawling's doing you no favors in your condition.

Let's just get to Grimfall as quickly as possible and hope she'll listen to reason."

* * *

Nelly, Eva, and Ana entered the Communicarium after traversing the path laid out for them by Grimfall. The cavernous room consisted of a catwalk suspended over a pit filled with five-foot-tall cylindrical devices. Nelly realized they were hundreds of large batteries. There was a curved glass ceiling, on top of which stood a gargantuan parabola with a rod protruding upwards from the center into the sky.

The catwalk rested on vertical and horizontal tracks which presumably would allow it to move all over the room. It enlarged into a circle in the middle before narrowing again on the other side of the room. Victoria Grimfall sat alone in the circle in her wheelchair.

"She's alone," Nelly marveled.

"Don't believe that for a second," Eva cautioned. "This is the most obvious trap I've ever seen. We'll go over there. *Cautiously.* I'll take point and put a bullet in her head if she tries anything." To Grimfall, she said, "The kid needs a doctor! She was injured by that poor girl you brainwashed. She won't last much longer."

"There will be no doctor," Grimfall replied. "Anastasia Romanov dies here. I have elected to take a risk by not letting her be treated. The only question is *how* she will die."

Eva yelled, "You heartless bitch! I'll end you myself!"

But Ana said, "No." By this point, she had lost all color on her face and trembled uncontrollably, yet a fire still burned in her eyes.

Eva gaped at her. "What do you mean, 'No'?"

"I won't hide behind you now that we've found our enemy. I will face her head on."

"Don't be stupid! She wants you dead, remember?"

Ana shook her head. "I don't care. I won't cower from her."

Eva emitted a loud, drawn-out sigh. "God dammit. Fine. Maybe a revolver in her face will make her change her mind. But I'll be right behind you, guns drawn, just in case."

"Thank you, Miss Eva. You're very nice." She curled her mouth into a grin. "For a Hapsburg."

"The cheek!" Eva shot back. But she, too, smiled.

They made their way forward across the catwalk. It was only wide enough for one person to walk, so they went single file. Eva had her revolvers drawn and she held them in front of Ana over the latter's shoulders, ready to fire. Ana kept stumbling and had to keep her hands on the railing to stay upright, but she managed to keep going.

About a third of the way to Grimfall, a large screen on the wall to their left turned on and a strange scene began playing out. People were lined up against a wall in a dark basement. A shocked Nelly realized they were the Romanovs. Ana stared horrified at the footage.

Within moments, soldiers entered the room and opened fire, cutting down the royal family. Nelly stood aghast as her stomach churned again. "You're a monster, Grimfall!" she shouted.

Grimfall simply said, "Keep watching."

"For the love of God, why?" Eva said. "It isn't enough you want to kill this kid. You have to also torture her by showing her the death of her family?"

"I don't understand," Ana said through heavy, rapid breaths. "There weren't any cameras in there."

The scene abruptly cut to another one. This time, Red Army troops drove up to the front of a mine and began unloading the bodies of Ana's family. Only...

"Ana! It's you!" Nelly said.

Ana's lifeless body was taken out of the truck and carried into the mine where it was buried in the floor.

"That doesn't make sense!" Ana said.

"You said you escaped from the truck after surviving the assassination attempt. When did they take you to a mine?" Nelly said.

"They didn't!" Ana said. "That never happened."

"Oh, but it did!" Grimfall said. "Just not in this world."

"What are you talking about?" Ana said. They had all stopped in their tracks upon seeing the footage.

Grimfall replied, "I suspect Eva Lamarr knows. About the Plurality of Worlds. After all, Farahilde Johanna certainly knew about it."

"What does she mean?" Nelly said.

Eva frowned. "It's... complicated. Kid, do you remember? When we first met, I told you Jeanne d'Arc unleashed a mysterious power and split the timeline in two."

"Yeah... kind of?"

"Well, supposedly that power came from God."

"What? The tree?"

Eva shrugged. "Who knows? Maybe it was the tree, maybe it wasn't. At any rate, Jeanne d'Arc got a power called the God's Body. She used it to win battles against the English in the Hundred Years'

War. But ol' Heavenly Father decided she was to be burned at the stake. Jeanne tried to be brave, but she ultimately used the God's Body to fight against her fate and escape from the English. This caused time to split in two, resulting in our world and another one where poor Jeanne was roasted alive."

Nelly's head spun. "Two worlds? Do you mean to say there are two of each of us?"

"I know there are duplicates of some people, but I don't know about everyone," Eva said.

Nelly shouted to Grimfall, "If there's a whole other world, why don't you look for a cure over there?"

"I did," Grimfall said. "They don't have one, either. In fact, they are a full century behind us technologically. And as you can see, Anastasia Romanov is dead there."

Eva, who had not lowered her weapons, said, "I should put you down here and now."

"You must not. There are very few people alive that understand the technology we created. If I die, the world will regress. Technological advancement will stagnate."

"Better that than murdering an innocent girl!"

"Perhaps you are right," Grimfall said. "In that case, I offer young Anastasia a choice." With a lethargic hand, she gestured to what appeared to be a doctor's scale next to her. It was a square platform just large enough for one person to stand on, and it had two metal bars rising vertically from the base. Cables ran from the thing up to the ceiling and into the parabola on the roof. "My time is almost up, and I may not live long enough to study the grand duchess' brain. Fortunately, I built a Plan B for this scenario and re-purposed my communications array. The antenna rising from the roof is an extremely powerful amplifier. It can enhance and 'broadcast'

Anastasia's healing power to the entire world. All ailments and injuries on Earth would be cured at once. The strain would kill her, but she's dying anyway.

"What will it be, Anastasia Romanov? Heal the world long-term, or heal everyone *now?*

"That's a shit choice!" Eva said.

But the doctor said, "Think about it. In the other world, you died for nothing and accomplished nothing. Here, you can make one of the largest contributions to humanity in recorded history and be remembered for all time."

"I've had enough of this!" Eva cocked her revolvers and zeroed in on Grimfall.

However, Ana grabbed her arms and held them away from Grimfall. "Wait!"

Eva gaped at her. "Are you out of your mind? It's like you *want* to die!" Ana began staring at the bizarre machine next to Grimfall. "Good God! You're not actually considering it, are you?"

"I..." Ana gulped. "I just watched the other Anastasia die a meaningless death. My chances of leaving here alive are exceedingly slim. This way, I can make a difference in the world."

Exasperated, Eva said, "You don't have to do this, kid. We can still force Grimfall to summon a doctor."

Ana shook her head. Her eyes were watery, now. "No. There's no time. I can feel it. I won't last more than another few minutes. I will make the sacrifice for all mankind."

Now, Nelly, had tears coming down. "Are you sure about this?"

"Yes. Please let me through, Miss Eva."

Eva put on a tough façade, but Nelly could tell she, too, was sad about this. "Fine. Do whatever you want."

She scooched back against the catwalk railing, allowing Ana to squeeze by. Ana went to the circle where Grimfall sat. "What do I have to do?"

Grimfall explained, "It's very simple. Just stand on the platform there and grip the handles. Once you squeeze the handles, it will activate. If it's any consolation, you'll feel no pain."

"If I do this, you must allow Nelly and Eva to leave here safely, along with Grigori Rasputin's body. And Alyona Petrov; let her return to her family."

Grimfall gave a pained nod. "You have my word. In a strange way, I must admit to a certain level of respect for your friends. They risked their lives to save you. And Alyona was only the means to get you here; I have no more use for her."

"Some of them did more than *risk* their lives," Ana reminded her.

"Indeed," Grimfall said. "The slovenly brute proved surprisingly resilient."

Ana glared at her but stepped onto the contraption. She spared one last look at her friends. "Thank you for everything you did for me. Nelly. And Miss Eva."

"I wish we could have done more," Nelly said sadly.

"It's fine," Ana said. "This is for the best."

Eva said, "You've got a lot of guts, kid. For a Romanov." She smirked.

Ana smiled. "And you were pretty nice. For a Hapsburg."

"I'll make sure the whole world knows what you did here," Eva said.

"So will I," Nelly said. "It'll be on the front page of my paper."

"Thank you." Ana turned her attention to the metal bars. She held out trembling hands and for a moment, it looked like she wouldn't go through with it. But she took a deep breath and gripped the bars. Her eyes went wide as a hum emitted from the pit below. It rose in intensity before becoming a deafening shriek.

Nelly wanted to put her hands over her ears but decided she shouldn't give any thought to her own comfort while Ana sacrificed her life for the whole world.

Nelly was startled by twin bolts of lightning that shot up from the base of the platform. Ana abruptly stiffened and stared into an unknowable future with vacant eyes. The lightning traveled up the cables and into the parabola. A multitude of yellow lights lit it up, and it began rotating back and forth until it settled upon what Nelly could only assume was the correct angle.

Something powerful rocked the *Potential*, and Nelly and Eva barely managed to grab hold of the railing to avoid being thrown off the catwalk. Up above, the parabola shook violently, and a wave of incandescent rainbow light shot from the tip of the rod in all directions.

Nelly turned her attention to Grimfall to see if she had been thrown off the catwalk, but the doctor's wheelchair had clamped onto the floor and was stable.

* * *

A river. That was the aptest description, although not the most scientific. A river of warm, cascading energy washed over Victoria Grimfall. She could feel herself gaining weight as her muscles returned to her. Her eyesight was enhanced to pre-ALS levels. The constant fatigue lifted off her and the rapturous energy of youth took hold once again.

Grimfall was overcome with unfiltered jubilation. She had solved her problem and beaten death. She no longer needed to rob and kill to stay alive.

But she *had* robbed and killed, hadn't she?

* * *

A startling change came over Grimfall. She seemed to increase in mass and looked increasingly less gaunt as the moments passed. Her expressions also became more animated, and a jubilant smile took hold. She ripped the cords out of her body with now-fully-functional hands. After about a minute she rose from the chair and stretched everything she could possibly stretch. This was the first time Nelly had seen her standing upright since 1889.

In fact, Victoria Grimfall now looked twenty years younger than she had as of late. The doctor celebrated with a maniacal laugh.

In contrast, Ana remained deathly still, still gripping the bars, her vacant eyes staring into an abyss. She stayed upright, impossibly stiff.

Eva ran over to her, and Nelly followed. When Eva made it to Ana, she said, "She's dead." Eva began trying to pry Ana's hands off the bars. "Rigor mortis has already set in." She turned her attention to Grimfall who seemed to be in a trance. "Get someone up here to help us! We're not leaving her like this!"

"Y-Yes, of course." She bent down and pushed a button on her wheelchair. "I need assistance in here."

Several burly men soon arrived, and they managed to pry Ana's hands free one finger at a time. Eva took her in her arms and put her down on the floor.

"She was so brave," Nelly said softly. She was deflated and almost lacked the energy to speak.

Eva closed Ana's eyelids. Without taking her eyes off the former grand duchess' immobile form, she said, "Tell me something, Grimfall. Anastasia Romanov gave her life for the entire world. Would you ever do the same? Is there anyone you care enough about to make the ultimate sacrifice for?"

Grimfall was silent for a long moment. Then, "No."

Eva continued, "Everyone has to die eventually. Sooner or later, you'll have to face your mortality again. When that happens, I wonder—will you have even a fraction of the courage this kid had?"

"Probably not," Grimfall admitted, her face a grim mask.

"Shut off the energy web. We're leaving," Eva said.

"Very well." She pushed another button on her wheelchair, and the web dissipated from the sky above. "You also could have destroyed a few Tesla Towers to make a hole in the web since they're what generate it."

"Yeah, thanks for finally telling us that, bitch. We'll also need to contact our friends so they can pick us up... if that's not *too much trouble.*"

"We'll return Alyona to her family. Zenaida must be worried sick," Nelly said.

Grimfall said, "I have a question for you two. You barely knew Anastasia Romanov. Why did you fight so hard for her?"

"Because people who barely knew *me* fought so hard for me a long time ago," Nelly replied, looking at Eva.

Grimfall said to Eva, "And why do *you* fight so hard for people you barely know?"

Eva scooped up Ana in her arms and rose to her feet. "Over a century ago, our ancestors displayed the power of the human spirit. Farahilde Johanna; Jeanne de Fleur; Gabrielle Deschanel; their examples continue to shape us and carry on into the future. I think... if this continues, it could snowball, and tomorrow's world will be a beautiful place. Maybe that's what God or the tree had in mind this whole time.

"In any event, everyone's been given an unbelievable gift today. You'd better not let it go to waste."

"I won't," Grimfall said. "I'm going to finish what I started and make the world a utopia."

"If you were right about the amplifier, then Ana just wiped out all disease on Earth, so that's a good start," Nelly said.

"It will be a while before we know for certain. It was built solely for Anastasia Romanov, so I couldn't test it beforehand. But if I was correct in surmising her true potential, she didn't just eliminate diseases. All injuries will have been healed, all missing limbs will be restored, and all deformities removed. If my amplifier succeeds in reaching all corners of the globe, everyone will be made equal."

Nelly said, "And yet, I can't help but wonder if it was all worth—"

She was cut off by another thunderous rocking of the *Potential*.

"Did the amplifier start up again?" Eva said.

Grimfall replied, "That's impossible without Anastasia Romanov."

Nelly pointed to the windowed ceiling. "Look!"

Dozens of crimson aeroships flew overhead, their lightning weaponry crashing against the *Potential*. Grimfall's ship shook violently, and they all had to grip the railings for support. "It's the Red Army!" the doctor said.

"They still want Ana," Nelly said.

"Either that or they don't fancy Grimfall's intrusion into their country," Eva said. "Let's get the hell out of here. Clownface! Where can our aeroship still dock with the *Potential?*"

"'C-Clownface'? Well, hmmm... there's another dock on Deck 50. I'll contact the *Philistine* and let them know you're coming."

Sighing, Eva said, "That's not its name anymore, but okay. Keep those Red Army knobs off us while we board our ship. Let's go!"

The canopy window overhead shattered under the assault of a white-hot tendril of electricity. Everyone had to scramble to avoid hundreds of falling daggers of glass. Many of the shards fell into the pit and punctured the batteries, causing them to explode in showers of sparks. This set off a chain reaction of bursting batteries. Nelly and Eva rushed across the catwalk and out of the Communicarium.

Glava 15

"Good, we lost them," Jay said. He and Michael continued to pilot the *Spring Hope*. They were well outside Moscow now, and the *Potential's* attack craft had broken pursuit. Now, Jay and Michael hovered above Losiny Ostrov National Park to the northwest of the city.

"Yes, but we will certainly find them again when we go back," Michael said.

The communications console began buzzing. "Maybe that's them," Jay said.

He went over and pressed the "Receive" button. "Nelly, Eva, is that you?"

"No, this is Victoria Grimfall." Jay's heart sank.

"What have you done with our friends?" he said.

"They are fine. Well, half of them. They're heading for Deck 50 to rendezvous with you. I'm transmitting the exact location of the dock to you now. Please hurry as we are under attack by Red Army forces."

"Why should we believe anything you say?" Jay said.

She groaned. *"What would be my motivation for lying to you? Why would I set a trap when I've already gotten Anastasia Romanov? Our business is concluded, so come and get your friends. Grimfall out."*

Jay returned to his station. "She said half our friends are fine. *Half.*"

"Regrettably, she must have succeeded in killing young Anastasia. I mourn for her, but we still have a duty to safeguard whatever friends remain."

"Right. Let's get over there."

* * *

The *Potential's* interior was abuzz with mad panic. Everyone scrambled every which way to either get to safety or their stations. Eva had to shove people aside when they blundered her way.

Nelly and Eva ran at a death-defying pace through the darkened corridors of the gargantuan aeroship. They had finally reached Deck 50, and Nelly was now sucking air, her lungs on fire. Her legs could more accurately be described as spaghetti at this point.

The airlock lay about a hundred yards in front of them, but Nelly grew more sluggish with each step. The aeroship was abruptly rocked by another attack from the Red Army ships swarming around outside. Nelly stumbled forward, and only Eva's quick thinking saved her from planting her face on the floor. Eva grabbed her arm to keep her upright, Eva's other hand on the railing which lined the hallway and no doubt had been installed for a situation such as this.

"Thanks!"

"Thank me after we're a thousand kilometers away from this hell. Can you make it?"

"I will," Nelly said, huffing and grunting. "No matter what it takes, I'm getting back to my family."

Eva took Nelly's right arm and draped it over the Austrian's shoulder. Nelly felt ashamed Eva had to carry her; she had always admired the Hapsburg's strength and endurance and wanted to pull her own weight. But at the end of the day, Nelly hadn't been prepared for this adventure, and Eva was *always* prepared.

As if sensing her thoughts, Eva said, "Don't feel bad, kid. You did well to make it this far. You've always had it in you to survive."

"I just wish I was as strong as you," Nelly said.

They plodded toward the airlock, one foot in front of the other, step by step. "Who says you're not? Anyone else would have been killed in the first few minutes of this nightmare. You were brave, determined, and quick on your feet throughout this show of shit. And, hey—think of the story you'll tell your kid when you get back."

"Heh. I guess you're right. Thanks."

"What did I tell you about thanking me? We could die within the next few moments."

"All the more reason to thank you before I lose the chance."

"Touché."

Something exploded behind them, and now a fire filled the rear of the corridor, meaning there was no turning back. *Thank you for making my point, life.* Smoke began filling the hallway, causing the two women to cough. Nelly grit her teeth as unbearable heat assaulted her in waves. She resolved to focus only on getting to the airlock.

"Just a few more feet!" Eva said.

A few agonizing moments later, they arrived. "Oh, no!" Nelly said.

The door was locked with a keypad. Grimfall hadn't said anything about needing a code to open it. "Well, shit," Eva said.

There was an intercom next to the door. Eva pressed the button. "Clownface! What is the blasted code?" No answer. "Answer me, or so help me God, I will come back from the dead and haunt you for all eternity!"

The speaker crackled. Someone was speaking on the other end. "I can't hear you!" Eva said.

"I... cod... nter... *5179.*"

"5179!" Nelly said.

Eva tried punching in the numbers, but there was a problem. The screen kept flickering, almost certainly the result of a compromised electrical system. Every time it did, it reset. *"Gott verdammt,"* Eva muttered. Meanwhile, the smoke continued to build within the confined space, and their coughing intensified. Nelly's eyes started to water.

Eva continued her attempts to punch in the numbers.

51—

Reset.

517—

Reset.

517—

Reset.

"Let me try it," Nelly said. "I'm a pretty good typist."

"Be my guest," an exasperated Eva replied in between coughs.

Nelly had been watching the flickering. The screen would stay lit up for one second before going dark for five. She placed her finger on the "5" button while it was still offline and concentrated all her mental energy on punching in the numbers as fast as humanly possible. Time seemed to slow down while she did this.

The screen lit up again and she hit all the required numbers like a woman possessed—because she mostly was. A friendly chime sounded, and the door began opening.

However, it quickly stopped when the panel reset again. Nelly screamed, raising her voice to a level it hadn't gone to since their 1889 adventure. She then caught herself and stopped, embarrassed.

"Come on, I think we can pry it the rest of the way!" Eva said. Nelly fumbled for the door; at this point, her vision had gone dark. Her hands fell on Eva's as the latter had already grabbed the door. Nelly moved hers lower and did the same. "Let's put everything we've got into one shove! On the count of three! One... two... three!"

Nelly screamed again, but this time it was in monumental exertion. Her muscles seemed to catch on fire, but she paid it no mind. She must have resembled a mental patient with the number of teeth she bared at that moment. And although she couldn't see Eva, the Austrian's bestial grunting told her she was putting just as much effort into it.

Little by little, they forced the door open enough so they could squeeze through. Eva let Nelly go first. Nelly couldn't even see what she was stepping into.

The voice of Grimfall suddenly sounded above her: "We managed to re-route power to your section."

Her vision brightened, and she realized the lights had turned on. Hydraulics sounded behind her along with the *shmf* of a closing door. All the smoke was sucked out of the airlock.

Eva patted her on the back. "Great job, kid."

"I couldn't have done it without you. Tha—"

It's still too early to thank her. They hadn't escaped yet.

"Give it a moment," Grimfall said via the intercom. "Your aeroship has docked but we need to synchronize air pressure."

Nelly took the opportunity to collapse to the floor. Eva said, "What's the situation like outside?"

"The Red Army has come in full force. Our weaponry has done a fair job keeping them at bay, but we are greatly outnumbered. We're focusing our fire around your location, but I can't guarantee the Reds won't break through."

"Can't you keep them out with your energy web?" Eva said. Nelly couldn't ask any questions herself as she had to fight for every breath.

"No, that has a minimum height which we are well below. However, once you're free of the *Potential,* ascend to a height of two thousand feet and we will re-activate it, thereby cutting off the enemy's pursuit." Another chime sounded. "Air pressure synchronization complete. You may leave now."

Eva said to Nelly, "Come on, kid. Let's go."

But Nelly had a new problem. "I can't get up. I don't have the energy."

Eva bent down. "Take my hand, then."

Nelly did so, and Eva pulled her to her feet and carried her out.

* * *

Nelly staggered into the cargo hold of the *Spring Hope* assisted by Eva. They headed straight for the bridge whereupon Nelly dropped into the nearest chair completely spent.

"Welcome back, Miss Eva," Michael said. "I take it things did not go your way over there."

"Couldn't be helped. The kid got injured and wouldn't have made it, so she decided to make her death count."

"What does that mean?" Jay said while seated at the controls.

"I'll explain later. For now, get us to two thousand feet."

The *Spring Hope* tilted backward as Michael and Jay angled her for an ascent. Outside, Red Army aeroships crowded the sky and exchanged electrical barrages with the *Potential*. Numerous explosions lit up the view outside the canopy window like fireworks. The *Potential's* hull had been heavily scorched by enemy fire and dozens of its cannons were now reduced to sparking stubs.

Nelly was pressed back into her seat by the very welcome G-forces. This meant they were getting out of here. However, despite being strapped in, she was flung to the side of the chair by a thunderous blow from the enemy. The ship stalled.

Eva ran over and worked the controls, her hands almost a blur. Nelly was thrust backward again when the engines restarted. The ship resumed its ascent, only whatever Eva had done had turned it into a rocket and now Nelly found her vision full of dark spots while they blasted into the heavens.

* * *

"Hey, kid! You all right? Come back to us!"

Nelly opened her eyes. Eva, Michael, and Jay stood around her. Her stomach twisted with nausea. "W-What happened?"

"You passed out," Eva said. "Sorry about that, but as it was an emergency, I activated the emergency boosters."

Nelly massaged her temple. "The Red Army...?"

They all smiled. "Rest assured, we 'gave them the slip' as you humans like to say," Michael said.

Jay nodded. "As soon as we got to two thousand feet, the energy web came on again and stopped the Red Army from continuing the chase."

"Then... it's over?"

She expected them to notify her of some new complication, but Eva said, "That's right, kid. Next stop: Vienna. I'll call in some favors and we'll get you home."

Nelly grinned. "Well, then, now I can say it. Thank you. All of you."

"Thank nothing of it," Michael said. "It is what we do."

"And we should be thanking *you* for bringing us together again," Jay said.

"It was good seeing you three after all these years," Nelly said. "I just wish we had gotten a happier ending."

Everyone became somber again. "Eva told us what happened. I'm sorry," Jay said.

Nelly explained, "Ever since that moment, I've gone back and forth with myself. Should we have stopped Ana? Part of me thinks so, but then, would she have died for nothing?"

Michael said, "We have been getting inundated with numerous broadcasts and other forms of communication. Young Anastasia's sacrifice seems to have paid off, for people everywhere are reporting their illnesses and injuries have been miraculously healed. It remains to be seen if Grimfall's machine reached the rest of the world, but at least here in Russia, the grand duchess is being hailed as the Motherland's greatest hero. Err, *heroine.*"

"Of course, Clownface couldn't resist the chance to brag. She's been telling everyone what happened," Eva said. "That's how she got the Red Army to back off. Victoria Grimfall is now viewed almost as much of a savior as the kid. Everyone's conveniently forgotten about the trouble she caused beforehand."

Nelly shrugged. "The needs of the many, and so forth."

"You know," Jay said, "Jeanne de Fleur liked to say the true power of the human spirit is living when all you want is death. Maybe we should add an addendum to that. 'The true power of the human spirit is living when all you want is death. But great power is also shown in bravely facing your own mortality.'"

"A little wordy, but I like it," Eva said.

Nelly stood up. "Okay, I need some proper rest now, so I'll be heading to my quarters."

"Go ahead, kid. You earned it."

Glava 16

Consciousness gradually popped back in like pieces of a puzzle. The last thing she remembered was grabbing the bars of Grimfall's machine. She put her hands on her stomach where her mortal wound had been, but her flesh was untouched now, leaving no evidence anything had happened.

Anastasia's eyes adjusted to the brightness, and eventually, an infinite white void spread out before her. It was not empty, however, as an impossibly large tree rose into the heavens to her right.

Standing in front of it were three women. One was dressed in a suit of armor, while another wielded a gauntlet with blades sticking out of it. The third woman resembled the armored one, just without the armor. Both had auburn hair, although the armored woman wore it in a braid while the plain-clothed lady had hers hanging free. The woman with the gauntlet had short, raven-black hair with dual cowlicks that resembled cat ears.

As if sensing Anastasia's presence, the trio turned around. "Well, well," Cowlick said. "The guest of honor has arrived." She looked like Eva Lamarr and had the same Austrian accent.

"Welcome, Anastasia Romanov," the armored woman said.

The plain-clothed woman said nothing.

"What is this place?" Anastasia said.

"When I was alive, I believed in Heaven," the armored woman said. "But first thing's first. My name is Jeanne de Fleur, my Austrian friend is Farahilde Johanna, and the third member of our

179

group is Gabrielle Deschanel. She doesn't speak much."

"The others mentioned you three. All of you lived a long time ago. Then, I must be dead." Grimfall had been right; Anastasia had not suffered when she died.

"Don't look so down, *mädchen*," Farahilde said. "You saved millions of lives with your sacrifice."

Jeanne nodded. "That was an incredibly brave thing you did."

"Oh, but we haven't answered your question. Allow me to explain. The universe has three layers to it. Creatura—Earth, the living world—is on the bottom, and Pleroma lies directly above it and intersects with it at certain points."

"Pleroma? That's the realm of the Gnostagar," Anastasia said.

"Yes," Jeanne said. "But resting above even that is this realm, Ennoea."

"And that green bastard behind us is Aeon, the, errrr, I guess you could call him the manager of this place," Farahilde said.

"Welcome, Anastasia!" a booming male voice called out.

"Who said that?" Anastasia said.

"It is I—Aeon. It is good to make your acquaintance."

"Okayyyy. If you're a manager, what do you manage?"

"I manage everything. It is the task for which I was created."

Anastasia's head started spinning as she struggled to understand the tree's words. "Were you created by God?"

"Who is God? *What* is God? Does the chicken come before the egg? Perhaps causality is a mere suggestion. Even I have a difficult time understanding the process. Either God created Man, or Man created God. But given that we cannot say for certain who is who, I would call it a moot point.

"At some point in the distant past, I became aware of my own existence. Along with that awareness came the knowledge I had a duty to manage everything. I took on the role of various deities for humanity to test out which one you were most receptive to. I could not decide on a clear winner, so I kept the religions separate.

"However, one day I made a critical mistake. I entrusted Jeanne d'Arc with great power, but I put too much pressure on her, and when that pressure broke her, reality was split in two and the parallel worlds went down different paths. Now doubting myself, I did not know which path was best.

"Ultimately, I decided upon an experiment. I would focus on this world—which I dubbed the Infini Calendar—and let the other one manage itself. Would a world without a manager do better or worse?"

"I-I see," Anastasia said. "And... what did you discover?"

Up until now, Aeon had been very serious. But now, he chuckled. "To put it simply, I discovered humans will follow their beliefs no matter how much I try to interfere. Neither world is perfect, yet neither is without hope. I tried to create a paradise with the Infini Calendar, and I may yet succeed, but perhaps there was no need. Mankind has proven itself capable of forging its own path.

"So, from this point forward, I will meddle no more."

Anastasia didn't fully understand, but she supposed things would be all right. "Well, ummm, thank you. But what happens now?"

"Now?" Farahilde said. "Now your family's waiting for you."

* * *

Liezen, Austria, the next day, noon.

The picturesque municipality of Liezen lay between the peaks of Salberg and Hirschriedel. Blue skies and sunshine were a fitting reward for their labors, Nelly thought.

They presently stood in a field outside town. A long-range aeroship, the *Schnellflügel,* had been summoned by Eva to take Nelly back to America. It resembled an ordinary aeroship, but it could be distinguished by its four engines instead of the normal two.

The *Schnellflügel's* ramp descended, and Nelly addressed her friends, perhaps for the last time. "Well, I guess this is it. It was, uh, really good seeing you guys again."

"It was good seeing you as well," Michael said, smiling. They *all* smiled.

"You really brought us together again, Nelly," Jay said.

"Get over here!" Eva said. The four of them hugged it out for a full minute. When they were done, Eva said, "I'm gonna miss you, kid."

The sniffles crept in. "I'm going to miss all of you more than you will ever know."

"Hey, maybe we'll meet again as senior citizens," Jay said.

"Michael's already a senior!" Eva joked about the immortal in their midst.

"I carry it very well."

The *Schnellflügel's* steward appeared at the top of the ramp and motioned for Nelly to board. "Take care, everyone," she said.

In response, her three friends saluted her.

Nelly ascended the ramp, and a cool breeze swept through her hair. She was finally returning to her family. New York.

Home.

She pulled out the insanely valuable gem Ana gave her and reflected on the friendship they had shared, however briefly.

A bittersweet smile touched her lips.

Epilog

A few days later, Grimfall gathered her board of directors for a debriefing in the conference room at Bronte-Astrope Marine Base #2 off the coast of San Francisco. The *Potential* had docked for badly needed repairs, and this seemed like a good time to catch up with her people.

"Everyone, our mission was a complete success. I am fully healed, as is everyone else on the planet."

"We are very happy you will continue to be with us," Tesla said while seated across from her at the long table.

"Indeed," Akira Kogishi said while seated at the end. "I just wish you had told me you were going to murder a teenager." Despite being in her eighties, the Japanese engineer remained as fiery as ever. She currently wore a light-blue turtleneck and dress pants, a fashion style she had picked up decades earlier. In addition, her hair was now completely white, yet her face remained remarkably devoid of wrinkles.

"You would have tried to stop me had you known," Grimfall replied.

Akira slid a newspaper over to her. "I would have never joined you *in the first place* had I known about your past." She had learned English decades ago.

The front-page story—written, of course, by Nelly Flowers—detailed Grimfall's exploits in Russia. But of more concern was Nelly's exposé on the director's time working for Robert Stone. "I... don't know what to say." Her immediate instinct was to deny it, but that would keep her chained as the villain. "It's all true."

"You set mankind up to be enslaved by the Gnostagar. *We* risked our lives to stop them in 1853. *You* happily got in bed with them in 1889," Akira said.

"Her contributions more than outweigh her crimes," Tesla said.

"Oh? What are your criteria for weighing human lives?" Akira said. "I'll be blunt. The director is effectively a war criminal. I am calling for a vote of no confidence. As an executive at what I thought was a good company, I have that right."

The other board members murmured nervously and talked among themselves in hushed tones. But before they could agree to a vote, a clerk rushed in holding a piece of paper that he handed to Tesla. "Good God!" the vice president said.

"What is going on?" Grimfall said.

Tesla explained, "We have received a signal from the stars. An extraterrestrial intelligence has made contact after detecting the worldwide broadcast of Anastasia's powers."

"Incredible!" Grimfall said. "What do they want?"

"Their English is somewhat questionable, but it seems they wish to welcome us into the greater galactic community."

Grimfall burst into hysterical laughter. "It's finally happened! Humanity has advanced to the next stage!"

"So it would seem," Akira said. "But I wonder... who else is performing on that stage? Are they friendly? Or are they like you, Grimfall—willing to kill to achieve their goals? I think we should all be very concerned."

Spasibo za prochteniye etoy knigi, tovarishch.

*Want to know what happened in Japan? Sign up for my newsletter to receive the bonus novella *The Black Fleet.*

https://dl.bookfunnel.com/zmq3w45v20

The Game Called Revolution: Le Contrecoup

(Taking place between *The Game Called Revolution* and *Secrets of the New World*)

The Tuileries, Paris, France, May 10, 1790 (Infini Calendar), 2:30 p.m.

The two "guests" entered the throne room of the newly ordained emperor of France. The room, like all the others previously used by the now deceased monarchs, was opulent in its design. The walls and ceiling were decorated with paintings of angels and saints gallivanting around. A magnificent chandelier hung from the ceiling, while a plush red carpet went unappreciated by the newcomers.

"We are here, *Emperor,*" Jeanne de Fleur said testily. She no longer wore the armor of the *Ordre de la Tradition.*

"So, you are," Napoleon Bonaparte said. He sat comfortably on his new throne, a ghastly blue and gold affair with stars and a giant "N" in the center of the back. Above and around him, a red and blue rug/curtain hung from a giant fake crown. "What happened to your eyepatch?"

"I completed my mission. I don't need it anymore," was the reply.

The dais was flanked by a security team holding bayonets. A wise choice, Jeanne thought. Otherwise, she might have lunged at him on the spot. Unlike Robespierre's troops, the uniform of these men consisted of white pants, long white gaiters, and blue sleeves that ended in red cuffs.

"Tell us what you want," Pierre said while standing next to Jeanne. His Middle Eastern skin stood in stark contrast to the paler hues of everyone in attendance. He, too, now wore simple civilian clothing.

"Very direct. I appreciate that," Napoleon said. "Allow me to be direct as well. Jeanne de Fleur is the people's hero here in France. She overcame great odds to save Europe and remove Maximilien Robespierre's iron grip on this nation. To not utilize such a powerful tool would be criminal. I wish for *Mademoiselle* de Fleur to return to service and once again lead the Ordre. You will be well compensated, of course, and our country will have peace of mind knowing you're defending it."

In response, Jeanne unleashed a bitter laugh. "Have you lost your mind? You betrayed my brother and stood by his murderers! To think I would swear loyalty to you is an act of madness. Come, Pierre. Let us leave this place."

They turned to leave. However, Napoleon shouted, "Do not turn your backs on me! To do so is to make an enemy of the Empire!"

Jeanne scoffed. "'Empire'! That is what my beloved France has become."

As they walked through the halls of the Tuileries, Pierre said, "Are you sure it was a good idea to antagonize him?"

"He deserves far worse," she said. "Whether or not he actually struck Jean-Paul down, my brother's blood is on his hands."

"Fair enough. But we're right in the lion's den. We could be attacked at any moment, and it's just the two of us."

She shook her head. "There are too many people here in this building. The *Emperor* won't risk making a scene, especially since this is *our* city. Paris has acknowledged our contributions to its wellbeing."

Pierre chuckled. "That is certainly an understatement. They would accept you as empress without question if you wished."

"I will not become what I despise most," she reminded him. "But on a more pressing matter, we need to leave France."

He sighed. "Well, damn."

"We'll return to Pierret to pack our belongings and say our goodbyes to your family. Then, we'll travel to Calais and board a ship for England. From there, we'll secure passage on a ship bound for America."

"You've given this a lot of thought."

"And you haven't? This was practically inevitable."

"I remained... optimistic."

She said, "Caution always wins against optimism."

He couldn't argue with that. However, there was another aspect of their escape to consider. "What will we tell the rest of the Ordre?"

"Nothing. They'll be endangered by any information we give them. We have to cut all ties with France."

She knew this was devastating to him, but he held it in like the professional he was. It wasn't any easier for her, and her heart would have a France-sized hole in it.

Celeste.
Viktor.
Vincent.
Catherine.

Not to mention the people she had already lost: her parents; Jean-Paul; Eugène; the king and queen; Jacques du Chard; Hubert.

But at least she and Pierre could stay together.

"My one consolation is we'll never have to deal with Farahilde Johanna ever again," Pierre said.

Jeanne smiled. "I don't know. I developed somewhat of a liking for her."

They had to find levity where they could.

* * *

The village of Pierret, France, May 11, 1790 (Infini Calendar), 9:12 a.m.

Catherine Reims was crying. Jeanne had known this would be difficult, but reality could often trump expectations. Vincent—her husband, village leader, and Pierre's adoptive father—comforted her as best he could. They stood in the Reims' house around the kitchen table.

"It's not fair!" she said in between wracking sobs. "You defeated Robespierre. We should all be happy!"

"I know," Pierre said. "But this isn't a kind world, and if we're to live in peace, we have to leave. For your sake, as well."

"Why not band together again and depose Bonaparte?" Vincent said.

Jeanne explained, "We used up the bulk of our resources defeating Robespierre. We don't even have an aeroship anymore. In addition, many of the people we recruited for that battle died; we don't want any more blood on our hands."

A rumbling in the distance caught their attention. "We might not have a choice," Pierre conceded.

Within moments, a company of soldiers, horses, and steam cannons rode through the village. The four of them ran out to greet the intruders. Their leader, a man with pompoms signifying his experience, stood arrogantly atop his horse in front of the village fountain. Jeanne recognized him instantly. He had protected the king's aunts during the French Revolution and helped them to escape persecution. "I am Marshal Louis-Alexandre Berthier. Jeanne de Fleur, we are here to conscript you into the service of the Emperor. Come along peacefully and no one will be hurt." His uniform had a red sash, and he wore a blue bicorn hat with white fur.

Jeanne carefully examined the scene. She had been hoping for more time, but what could be done? They were at a severe disadvantage. She respected Berthier for his service to the throne, but he seemed to have changed since Napoleon seized power. Finally, she said, "I'm not going anywhere without my companion."

The 36-year-old Berthier turned up his nose at the mention of Pierre. "*Le Chevalier* Girard is not needed by the Emperor. You will come alone."

"Perhaps," Jeanne said. "But should he not be used as a hostage to assure my compliance?"

The Marshal was silent as he mulled it over. "Very well. It wasn't very smart of you to suggest that, though."

We shall see, she thought.

Pierre turned back to his adoptive parents. "Thank you for everything."

Catherine wailed as they led Jeanne and Pierre into a waiting prison steam carriage with no windows. Jeanne was put in the backseat next to a guard, while Pierre sat across from her next to his own guard. The procession then formed up and sped out of the village.

As they watched the forest shooting past them, Pierre said, "Drat. I could have stayed."

"As if I would let you abandon me," Jeanne said.

He suddenly raised his voice. "I was not given a choice in the matter!"

"I am your commander. You will do as I say," Jeanne said icily.

"I refuse!"

In response, she leaned forward and began raining punches on him. There was such a cacophony in the carriage that her guard had to put their hands on Jeanne to restrain her.

Suddenly, she elbowed him in the nose. A satisfying crunch resounded, and blood spurted out. The guard next to Pierre registered shock, but it was too late. Pierre grabbed his head, and Jeanne grabbed the head with the broken nose, and they rammed them into each other. Both soldiers slumped against each other and the door next to them.

Pierre smiled. "That was a nice lover's quarrel."

"You overestimate yourself if you think you've earned the right to call yourself my lover." But she smiled, too.

"We need to take out those two steam cannons. They'll annihilate us if we try to take off in this carriage."

"There will be one directly behind us and another at the front of the procession for good measure. There will also be calvary on either side of us," Jeanne said. "I'll go for the front cannon. You secure the one in the back. Try to cause as little bloodshed as possible."

"Will do, Commander. It's just like old times."

"The times aren't *that* old, Pierre."

As it turned out, Jeanne was correct about there being calvary directly outside. Its rider jerked his head to see why the door to the carriage was being opened. Instantly spotting Pierre, he removed his saber and slashed at the chevalier. However, his horse suddenly stumbled trying to avoid debris on the path they were traveling, and he struck a gash in the metal exterior of the carriage instead.

Holding onto the door support, Pierre extended a long leg and kicked the cavalryman off his horse. He then leaped onto the equine and turned his head to observe Jeanne doing the same thing on the other side of the carriage.

* * *

Satisfied that Pierre was handling himself without any problems, Jeanne sped forward on her horse. The scenery whipped passed them at a frantic pace. There had been six cavalrymen on either side of the carriage, which now left five for her to deal with. There was one behind her and four in front.

The horseman directly behind her wasted no time galloping over to subdue her. He reached out to grab her arm, but she hopped over to his horse and got behind him. She pulled his saber out of its sheath and put the blade to his neck. "Get next to the cannon up front!" she shouted to be heard over everything else.

With no other options, the soldier complied and whipped his steed to go faster. The cavalrymen in front must not have heard the commotion, as they were taken completely unaware. "Pull them down!" Jeanne said to her hostage. One by one, they rode up alongside the other riders and yanked them off their horses.

They were about a dozen feet from the steam cannon when the cavalrymen on the other side noticed what was going on. One of them rushed over to help his compatriot. The newcomer raised his rifle and aimed at Jeanne, apparently forgetting he was supposed to take her alive. Jeanne's prisoner frantically waved his hands to try and get his ally to re-think the situation, but it was no use. The man lined up his shot.

Jeanne removed the saber from her hostage's neck and hurled it at the cavalryman who was about to fire. The sword sliced through the air and split the rifle in half, barely missing its wielder. The brash cavalryman lost his balance and fell off.

With no more leverage against the man sitting in front of her, she simply grabbed his shoulder and shoved him off. She took the reins herself and got next to the steam cannon. The vehicle was a steam carriage with two enormous cylinders on top, each one big enough for an adult to crawl inside.

She leaped off the horse onto the roof and took hold of one of the cylinders before kneeling to examine its base. After her encounter with the steam cannon at Mt. Erfunden, she had made sure to always carry a certain set of tools. She removed a socket wrench from a secret pocket in her clothes and began working the sockets holding the cylinder in place. She laboriously moved her hand back and forth to remove them; within a few minutes, her arm was on fire.

Eventually, she tested the cylinder and now it was wobbly. Summoning all her strength, she pushed it to the left of the carriage. It soon gave with a screech that could be heard despite all the noise.

Her job done, she leaped off the carriage, tucking and rolling as she hit the ground.

The cylinder fell to the side of the carriage. It weighed upwards of three hundred pounds, so that threw the vehicle off balance. The carriage flipped over onto its back, kicking up a cloud of dust and shattering the windows.

Jeanne gingerly returned to her feet. She was getting too old for this. Despite everything, she looked forward to a life of peace after this was over.

The rest of the procession stopped immediately. The remaining two cavalrymen, along with several of the de-horsed ones, hurried up to her and readied their rifles. One of them was Berthier. "Well done, mademoiselle. Even I was somewhat entertained by that spectacle. However, this is the end of your resistance. We wished to be civil, yet regrettably, we must bound and gag you now."

"Perhaps you should think twice about that!"

The Marshal turned his head to see Pierre popping up from the top of the rear steam cannon. The color drained from his face as he realized he had lost the advantage—all of it.

"Get out of here," Jeanne said. "And for the record, it's *Commander*."

The soldiers turned their horses around. "On foot!" Pierre commanded. They reluctantly obeyed and Jeanne slapped the horses to send them running away. The soldiers followed in their wake, desperate to get away from the occupied steam cannon.

Jeanne got in the carriage next to Pierre. "Well done, Pierre."

He grinned. "Perhaps now I have gained the right to call myself your lover."

"We shall see. For now, we must get to Calais before Napoleon figures out our plan. He has a sharp mind, so it won't be long."

"Anything you say, milady," Pierre said, imitating Celeste.

"Now you've gone too far!" Jeanne laughed.

Within a day, they reached Calais and boarded a ship bound for America.

* * *

Hofburg Palace, Vienna, Austria, May 12, 1790 (Infini Calendar), noon.

Farahilde Johanna strolled through her family home in Austria. She had just returned from her mission to mete out justice against Maximilien Robespierre. Though this had been accomplished, her heart continued to ache at the loss of her beloved sister, Maria (more commonly known as Marie Antoinette by French worms everywhere). Maria had been her idol and favorite person in the whole world, so when she was taken prisoner by her subjects, Farahilde embarked on a campaign of death and terror to right that wrong.

Try as she might, though, she couldn't save Maria. The French monsters executed her without a second thought. Even Jeanne de Fleur had been caught off guard by the sudden turn of events orchestrated by Robespierre. They had all discovered too late the identity of their enemy.

But Farahilde Johanna wasn't known for forgiveness or mercy, so she teamed up with Jeanne and her knights to see to it her sister was avenged.

As she walked through the wide hall with its white walls, paintings on the ceiling, high windows, and numerous intricate golden chandeliers, the people stepped to one side and wouldn't look her in the eyes. They seemed even more afraid of her than usual.

At the end of the hall, her brother, Leo, awaited. As usual, he had a scowl on his face, so she couldn't tell if anything was different.

But when their soldiers appeared from both ends of the hallway, she knew things were very different, indeed. "I'm home, brother," she said in an attempt to look jovial.

"Yes, you are," he said. He wore his stupid white jacket, orange vest, and equally tacky blood-orange sash. His hair was that white abomination European royalty loved so much. "You've returned from your unauthorized leave after having murdered a foreign ruler."

"*Former* foreign ruler," she said. "In case you haven't heard, he'd been de-throned. By us. I had the new ruler's permission to carry out his *scheduled* execution."

He snarled at her as he talked. "That doesn't change the fact you went to another country and waged war against its legitimate government."

"*Legitimate government?* Maximilien Robespierre cruelly butchered our sister! He couldn't be allowed to continue breathing another moment."

"Enough! These men will escort you to a cell where you will await trial for the charges of desertion and murder." She tensed and prepared to fight by raising her bladed gauntlets. However, in a rare moment of clarity, she realized that would just make things worse. Instead, she raised her hands and allowed the guards to disarm her.

She didn't know what the future held, but she knew one thing to be certain: She would never, ever regret killing Robespierre.

* * *

The Tuileries, May 17, 1790 (Infini Calendar), 2:15 p.m.

Napoleon's new guest entered the throne room. Unlike Jeanne de Fleur, this one would be cooperative, even if she bore a strong resemblance to the former leader of the Ordre. Her hair was much shorter, but otherwise, she had the same height and body type as de Fleur.

"Gabrielle Deschanel, reporting as ordered," she said while keeping her hands behind her back standing at attention. She wore simple peasant clothing because her particular branch of the military had no uniform. Better to blend in that way.

Napoleon stood up to greet her. "Welcome, *Madame* Deschanel. I brought you here because I have a new assignment for you. I want you to take over for Jeanne de Fleur and lead the Ordre."

"With all due, respect, my Lord, I'm an assassin. I don't defend lives, I take them. I would be a poor substitute for the beloved Commander."

"You misunderstand," Napoleon said. "You're not going to replace her. You're going to *become* her. You will be Jeanne de Fleur in name and appearance. And is not one life saved by another life taken? By killing our country's enemies, have you not been defending it?"

He thought he detected a slight twitch in her features when he revealed his plans. It was probably nothing to worry about, though.

She remained stoic. "Very well, my Lord. I will assume the role of Jeanne de Fleur."

"There is no hurry," Napoleon said. "You'll have to grow your hair out, and we'll need to tailor an appropriate costume—nay, uniform. Good things take time."

Especially things like the legitimizing effect "Jeanne le Juste" working for him would have for his rule.

Continued in *Secrets of the New World (Infini Calendar #2)*, on sale now.

Sneak Peek: Moonlight Magic

This is the sequel to *Moonlight Crusade (Moonlight Chronicles #1)* which I published last year. It's the next book I'll be releasing (fingers crossed). Note: Unlike the Infini Calendar series, the Moonlight Chronicles series is for mature readers, as it contains graphic violence, strong language, and sexual content. Reader discretion is advised, although for this snippet I chose a few clean passages to share.

Angelica Brassi stood leaning against the white wall of St. Peter's Basilica that morning in Vatican City, deep in thought. The Renaissance building towered over St. Peter's Square, with the massive dome on top bringing the church's total height to 448 feet. She thought the size was an appropriate mirror for her troubles.

What concerned her were her recent actions regarding the Fatima prophecy. Yes, they had prevented the apocalypse, but doing so had required consorting with vampires. Specifically, Kyle Falconer and his friends. She had, in effect, deceived her superiors and spat on the Catholic faith by cooperating with unholy abominations. It was for the greater good, of course, but she couldn't help feeling tainted. Her duty told her to kill any undead monsters she encountered, but Falconer's curious quasi-manzil were shockingly non-threatening.

The problem was that they had applied to the Guide and had gotten accepted as an official manzil. Every Redeemer was taught that every manzil must be eradicated, and she had just helped a new one get established. Her superiors weren't fools; they spied on the Guide well enough to know when a new manzil is created. They hadn't said anything yet, but she feared they would soon want answers.

"Angelica!"

Speaking of wanting answers. Here came someone who wanted them more than anyone. Eve stormed over wearing her uniform which consisted of an unassuming black cassock with white bands on the forearms to indicate an apprentice. Angelica's uniform was the same except she had red bands. Eve had been trained quite well in recent weeks, though that didn't give her the right to speak to a Senior Purge Specialist this way.

They were all alone in the large square that later on in the day would hold thousands of tourists and the faithful. The Egyptian obelisk at the other end, which predated the square itself, shot into the sky like a beacon to Heaven. "I want an explanation," Eve said. At five-foot-nine, she was taller than many women at the Vatican. Her raven hair came down to her elbows. Her pouty cuteness was attractive to some of the men here. Angelica had caught them sneaking glances at Eve when her back was turned. God was mighty, but so were the Devil's temptations.

"I'm sure you do," Angelica said.

Eve pointed an accusing finger at her. "Why didn't you tell me my brother was alive? I have a right to know!" Her eyes burned with the fire of the wronged. Or, at least, those who *believe* they have been wronged.

"I made the call," Angelica said. "I felt you were better off not knowing what really happened to Kyle, and the higher-ups agreed."

Eve put a hand to her face to hide her tears. "So, it's true? My brother is a vampire?"

"Yes. I'm sorry, but yes."

Eve began sobbing. Angelica felt she should comfort her, but that was never one of her strengths.

Angelica Brassi dealt with bad situations, usually with death, but she couldn't make people feel better.

When Eve stopped crying, she sniffed the snot back into her nose and said, "I need to see him."

"That's impossible," Angelica replied. "The bishops will never allow it. As a vampire, Kyle Falconer is officially an enemy of God now."

"No!" Eve shouted. "Kyle's a good person! He's as Christian as any of us."

Angelica decided the best thing she could do for Eve was to admit what she could not admit to anyone else. "Yes, I know. I saw that firsthand. He's not evil, nor is anyone else in his manzil. But do you really think His Holiness will see a difference? To those that aren't on the front lines, every enemy must die. These are strange times we live in where vampires can be good."

Eve was silent as she seemed to mull something over. Then she said, "So, he has a manzil? A new family?" Her voice was strained as if that hurt more than his vampiric status.

"Yes. He lost everything and somehow managed to start anew. He has them now, and it would be best to let him go."

"Easy for you to say. There aren't any vampires in *your* family."

Angelica shrugged. "That I know of."

Eve continued. "I don't care what anyone says. Kyle's my brother, and I'm not abandoning him. I'll ask Goldie for help. Don't think I don't know what she does behind the scenes."

"We don't speak of such things," Angelica said. "Cooperation is sometimes needed, that's all. And anyway, what would you do even if you did get permission? A Redeemer who fraternizes with the undead would lose her standing here."

"Goldie hasn't lost her standing," Eve countered.

Angelica sighed. She didn't like having to speak of Goldie's activities. "The few people who know what she does understand she's using the Guide to further our own interests. She's a senior official. You would not be granted the same understanding."

Evidently deciding to switch tactics, Eve said, "Nobody has to know about this. I'll petition the Cloister to go home to pay my final respects to my brother. While in America, I'll go to New York and find him. Goldie's contacts must know where he is. Or maybe *you'd* like to tell me?"

"Forget it. I'll play no part in your schemes. They are—as you know—officially registered as the Greenwich Street manzil, but that street covers a lot of ground. I don't have to help you throw your reputation away by saying any more."

"Fine," Eve said. "I'll go to Goldie."

She turned to leave, but Angelica said, "Be careful around that one. Even I don't know what goes through her head."

Eve said nothing and simply left.

* * *

December 26th.

Ducane sat in his office going over paperwork. The Guide's unofficial enforcer had been busy lately with everything that had happened with the Kyrios manzil and the Grand Imam in New York. Although known as a brute and a thug, he still had his official duties to take care of. At the moment, he was writing a report on the formation of the Greenwich Street manzil.

His office was spartan in more ways than one. Besides his steel desk and rigid chair, the only other decorations in this room were ancient Celtic weapons that hung from the walls. He had wielded those very same instruments of war centuries ago. He kept them not just for nostalgia, but as a reminder to be ready to fight when necessary. Most of the time he was a pencil-pusher, so it was good to be reminded.

Sometimes he yearned to return to the old days of executing anyone who crossed the line. These days, *protocol* had to be adhered to. They hadn't listened to him when he warned them about Kyrios' activities and the world had almost ended as a result.

A red light on his desk went off with an annoying beep. That meant it was a Code Zero. Sighing, he pressed the button next to the light. This caused his door to be fully barred against entry because he didn't want anyone to see what was about to happen.

The wall to the right of his desk slid open to reveal a black screen. On said screen appeared a plus-sized young blonde woman wearing a nun's habit. He knew she was blonde because there were always bright strands sticking out from her attire. "Hello, luv!"

"Goldie," he said.

"Oof," she said. "Still got that scowl, have we?"

Grinding his teeth, he shot back with, "I wouldn't be scowling if you people hadn't mishandled the Grand Imam situation. You had all the intel you needed, yet you only spared a measly few Redeemers."

"We are sorry about that. Bit of a cock-up, that. Won't happen again. Promise!"

"Do I have your word, then, that when the next Kyrios appears, you won't foul it up?"

Her cheerful demeanor never wavered. "Perish the thought, luv! You can be rightly assured next time won't be a damp squib."

He groaned. "What do you want?"

"Oh, now, don't be like that. I'm bridging the gap between us, and I just got a special request that I need your help with."

The only reason he ever offered his help to her was that she often gave him information on what the Vatican was up to. "And just what is this 'special request'?"

She grinned even wider. "Well, a certain forlorn sister is looking to reunite with her dear brother. Poor sod got turned and now it's a messy situation."

"And what does this have to do with me?"

"The poor sod's name is Kyle Falconer, and I'm told you know where to find him."

Hmph. So, that was it. "Perhaps I do, but the official addresses of manzils are kept by the Guide, and we don't like giving them out for Redeemers eager to kill them."

Goldie held up a finger. "Ah, but I'm not a Redeemer. Just a faithful sister who occasionally names your wonderful abilities. I hear there's a new one where you attach strings of darkness to your fingers and slash with them. I think I'll call it 'Dark Hand.' Yep, think that'll go over real well.

"Oh, but that has nothing to do with what you said. Anyway, yes, Redeemers are involved, but there'll be no killing. It's just a simple reunion."

"It may be simple," Ducane said, "but that information will still cost you."

She put her hands together in a pleading gesture. "Of course, of course! I could give you the movements of a few Redeemers in and around Jerusalem. Should make things more secure for you over there, as long as you promise not to kill them. Questions would be asked, then. Questions I won't want to answer." At this, she finally dropped her smile.

Ducane cracked his neck to get rid of the stiffness that came with sitting in a chair all day. "I know how it goes. You have my word we will only watch them. But if *they* attack, things will be different."

The smile reappeared and she clapped her hands together. "Fabulous! In that case, we have a deal."

"Very well," Ducane said. "Kyle Falconer can be found at a bar on Greenwich Street called Marvelous Mel's. That is the official headquarters of his manzil."

"Excellent! I'll inform his sister promptly. Oh, and here are the names I promised you..."

Coming in 2023 (maybe).

Also by Scott Kinkade

God School (Divine Protector #1)

18-year-old Ev Bannen was just hoping to get admitted to college. He never expected to be recruited to a school for gods, where he'll be spending his days building up his strength, learning to answer prayers and getting an education in religion alongside aspiring god of money Jaysin Marx, the lovely but troubled Maya Brünhart and anger-prone ginger Daryn Anders. But when the world is threatened, Ev must step up to save the day.

Published December 9, 2014.

Amazon US: https://tinyurl.com/y9vy5xsy

Amazon UK: https://tinyurl.com/yaxu6mdq

Amazon CA: https://tinyurl.com/y7htn9ly

Moonlight Crusade (Moonlight Chronicles #1)

College student Kyle Falconer's trip to New York City gets a bloody extension when his Christian group is brutally murdered by vampires. Now undead himself, Kyle is taken in by a sympathetic woman with the ability to see the future, and she begins training him to defend himself against the madman who slaughtered his friends. With a holy war looming on the horizon, Kyle must gather allies to save the world while also dealing with Vatican vampire hunters and the undead Yakuza.

Contains graphic violence and strong language. Not for kids.

Published July 13, 2021.

Amazon US:
https://www.amazon.com/dp/B096R2JX1R

Amazon UK:
https://www.amazon.co.uk/dp/B096R2JX1R

Amazon CA:
https://www.amazon.ca/dp/B096R2JX1R